Summer W

Mountain Ridge R

By

Rose Bak

About This Book

This wedding is supposed to be a chance for her to finally make peace with her daughter, not fall in love with one of the guests...

Erika is thrilled when her daughter April invites her to her destination wedding at the Mountain Ridge Resort. After years of estrangement, the mother and daughter are finally finding their way back to a solid relationship. Erika fully intends to focus on her daughter April this weekend, not herself. She needs to show her daughter that she's no longer the selfish person she remembers from her childhood.

Reed never had time for love, but he has always enjoyed his role as the fun bachelor uncle to his sister's brood of kids. When the wealthy CEO arrives at the Mountain Ridge Resort for his nephew's wedding, the first thing he does is hit someone with his car. The second thing he does is fall in love with the mother of the bride.

She's sworn off love, but he's going to do his best to convince her that she deserves to take a chance on happiness...

"Summer Wedding" is a steamy standalone in the Mountain Ridge Resort series. This contemporary instalove romance includes a myriad of wedding disasters, a couple finding love in midlife, and matchmaking family members who won't stop until there's a happily ever after.

Summer is the season for love at Mountain Ridge Resort! Pack your bags and get ready to have the time of your life at this charming, lakeside resort nestled in the Virginia mountains. This summer, our guests are getting much more than they expect, when what starts as a summer getaway ends in love and happily-ever-after! Your reservation is confirmed. Check in today, and join some of your favorite romance authors for twenty-five unforgettable, steamy, summer love stories.

This book includes a special excerpt from "Until You Came Along", book one of the Oliver Boys Rockstar series, available now from all major online retailers.

Join My Mailing List

Click here[1] to join Rose Bak's mailing list. You'll get a free book and be the first to hear about all the latest releases and special sales.

Dedication

For everyone who has the courage to face up to their past mistakes and make things right.

Prologue—Erika

Six months ago...

"Mom! I'm getting married!"

My daughter's exuberant voice popped across the line the minute I picked up the call. I smiled, thinking that her happiness was contagious.

"Jonathon proposed? That's great honey! I'm so happy for you."

"We're having the wedding at the Mountain Ridge Resort in Virginia," April continued. "We were there for a wedding last summer and we both loved it. And best of all, they had a cancelation, so they were able to fit us in over Labor Day weekend."

"Wow, that's so soon."

"Jonathon's Uncle Reed is paying for a wedding planner as our gift. Apparently she's really good and she's worked on several weddings with the Mountain Ridge events planner so that will make everything a lot easier."

"That's very kind of him."

"Well, I was going to refuse, but he's rich—not that you would know that when you meet him because he seems way laid back and normal – and Jonathon's mom said we should let him help us. Anyway, we'll do the rehearsal Saturday and the wedding Sunday night. That way people can go home on Labor Day and not have to take another vacation day, unless they want to, of course."

"That's a great idea."

My daughter was always very thoughtful, something she got from her father.

"Does that weekend work okay for you Mom? It's about an eight hour drive from Manhattan. Will you have any problem getting there?"

My heart thudded in my chest.

"I'm invited?"

5

"Of course you are, Mom. Why wouldn't I want you to be there for my big day? You're the mother of the bride."

Tears filled my eyes. I couldn't believe my daughter had invited me to her wedding. We'd just started talking again about two and a half years ago after a lengthy estrangement, and things were sometimes a bit tentative with us. We were more like strangers than mother and daughter, especially when we'd first started talking again. Gradually we'd gotten to know each other again, and I think we'd both felt more comfortable around each other the last year.

I'd been working hard to show her that I wasn't the same selfish person I had been when she was younger, back when I had been deep in my addiction. I'd made it a personal mission to earn back her trust. April inviting me to the wedding was a dream come true. It signified that I'd earned her forgiveness and was important in her life again. I didn't deserve it, but I was immensely grateful for our new relationship.

"I will absolutely be there. I wouldn't miss your wedding for anything in the world."

Reed

"Uncle Reed, when will you get here?"

I smiled at Jonathon's eager tone, even though he couldn't exactly see me through the car dashboard.

"I'm pulling into the parking lot now," I told him as I swung into an open parking spot that came up unexpectedly. "I'll...oh shit!"

"What's the matter?"

"I need to go, I'll call you when I'm checked in."

I clenched the steering wheel and took a deep breath, raising my head to look at the woman who was now on the hood of my car. The very angry woman. Our eyes met through the windshield and for a moment I lost my breath. She was beautiful.

Mentally shaking myself, I turned off the car and got out. My heart was racing. I couldn't believe I'd almost hit someone. I hadn't even seen her.

"I am so sorry. Are you okay? Do you need medical attention?"

The woman made to roll off the hood of the car and I rushed over to help her. I took her hand and everything inside me stilled. *Mine.* The word reverberated through my skull as what felt like an electrical current traveled between our palms.

"Careful," I said softly, my voice rough.

The woman stood up, brushing off her clothing. She was about my age, late forties or early fifties, with a trim, athletic figure. Faded jeans lovingly hugged her slim legs and narrow waist, and her tank top showed toned arms and generous breasts that I was itching to get my hands on. She had thick brown hair that fell past her shoulders in a cascade. Her eyes were chestnut brown, huge in her pale white face, and she had the cutest little button nose. And then there was her mouth...pouty thick lips, slick with some kind of gloss, and pressed together in a frown that told me she wasn't happy.

Oh yeah, probably because I'd hit her with my car.

7

"Are you okay?" I asked again. "I'm not sure what happened."

Her eyes narrowed in a glare.

"You were driving too fast and too busy talking on your phone to notice I was crossing through this parking space," she told me. "I jumped up on the hood to avoid being crushed."

She pointed at the car in the spot in front of me. There was maybe six inches between the bumper of that car and mine. Jesus. If she hadn't jumped up I might have crushed her. Whoever this woman was, she had good reflexes. I felt sick to my stomach at the idea that I could have seriously hurt her by not paying attention.

"Are you injured?" I asked.

She looked thoughtful and I had the sense she was doing a scan of her body for injuries.

"Probably bruised but nothing's broken, thank God."

"Let me make this right," I said, giving her a smile that had melted a lot of panties in my forty-nine years on this Earth. "Can I buy you dinner later? Or maybe a drink after you check in?"

Her spine snapped straighter, and she gave me a glare that could melt steel.

"Are you seriously hitting on me after you damn near ran me over?"

"Oh. Ah. No," I lied. "I just...what can I do to make it up to you?"

"Watch where you're going next time," she growled. "The next person you try to run over might not be as lucky."

She bent over to pick up the suitcase that she must've dropped when she was evading my car, and I absolutely did not check out her heart-shaped ass. Without another word, she started to walk away at a fast clip.

"At least let me give you my phone number," I said, jogging to catch up with her. "You can call me if you need anything."

She picked up her pace. "Leave me alone, asshole!"

Raising the middle finger of one hand over her shoulder to let me know what she thought of me, she stormed off towards the Main Lodge.

I sat back down in my car, feeling shaken. I couldn't decide if it was because of the near-miss of hitting the woman, or if it was my response to the woman herself. Even angry and flipping me off, there was something about her that called to me. I'd never felt this way about anyone before.

And you let her get away, dumbass, I told myself.

I gathered up my suitcase and headed into the lodge to check in, my pulse still racing. The woman was clearly staying here, so I'd just have to keep a look out for her. If we were meant to be – and I had no doubt that we were – fate would bring her to me again sooner or later.

Erika

"Mom! You made it!"

I looked up from the resort map to see my daughter rushing towards me on the path. She pulled me into a tight hug, and I squeaked as she pressed against what I was guessing was a nice bruise forming on my side from where I'd landed on the hood of that guy's car. My knees and thighs were throbbing, telling me those were banged up too.

That guy, whoever he was, he might be a shitty driver, but he was hot as hell. I guessed he was close to my age, judging by the streaks of gray in his dark brown hair and neatly trimmed beard. Laugh lines had bracketed his almond shaped brown eyes. Even dressed in dress pants and a white button down shirt, it was obvious that he was lean and fit. I'd seen the bulge of his biceps as he'd helped me off the car, and I couldn't help but notice his flat abs and trim waist.

Unlike a lot of guys our age, he clearly took care of himself.

If I'd been here alone – and if he hadn't hit me with his damn car – I'd probably have thought harder about taking him up on his offer for dinner. The look of interest in his eyes was unmistakable, and I'd be lying if I said I hadn't felt the same glimmer of attraction. But I was here at the Mountain Ridge Resort for my daughter. There was nothing that would take my attention away from helping make her wedding weekend special.

April stepped back and I accepted a hug from her fiancé Jonathon, wincing when he inadvertently touched the sore spot. My daughter studied me, taking in the smudges of dirt on my shirt and jeans.

"Are you okay Mom?"

My first thought was that she was implying that I'd relapsed, but I pushed away that insecure thought. After eight years of sobriety, it wasn't impossible that I'd relapse, but it was much less likely than it had been in the early days after I'd first graduated treatment. April had seen how committed I was to staying clean. Her question must have come because she'd seen me wince in pain.

"I'm fine, someone just hit me with their car."

"What?!?!" my daughter screeched.

"Are you okay?" Jonathon asked at the same time. He looked like he wanted to go find the person and beat them up for me.

"Yeah." I shrugged dismissively, not wanting to make a fuss.

"Some asshole was talking on his phone and not looking where he was going. He pulled into a parking spot at a fast pace just as I was walking through it. I had to jump onto the hood of his car to keep from getting run over or crushed between his car and the one in front of him."

April put her arm around me. "Holy crap, that's scary. Are you sure you're okay? Maybe the resort has a nurse on site or something."

I nodded. "That's not necessary. I can feel a nice bruise coming up and I'm a little sore from landing on the car, but I'm sure I'll be okay after I take a hot bath. Don't worry."

"Do you want some ibuprofen or something?" April asked.

"No thanks. I don't take any painkillers, ever."

My daughter's cheeks reddened as she realized her faux pas.

Painkillers had been the start of my problems all those years ago. I'd been in a car accident that caused significant trauma to my back and neck. Back then, doctors had prescribed opioid pain medication like candy, and soon I was hooked on them, taking them by the handful. As my tolerance to the pain pills built up, I'd turned to alcohol and pot to help manage my pain and keep the high that I craved. Of course, I knew now it wasn't about the pain from the car accident. I was numbing the pain of something that had happened to me when I was much younger. But back then, I was sure the car accident injuries were my problem.

My husband, ex-husband now, had been a saint. He'd put up with me as long as he could, trying to get me help, but I wasn't ready. I thought I had a handle on everything. Him kicking me out and divorcing me wasn't rock bottom. Him getting full custody of April wasn't rock bottom either. Rock bottom had still been a few years away.

I pulled myself out of my maudlin thoughts and focused my attention on my daughter.

"What do you need help with, honey?" I asked.

"The wedding planner has everything under control I think," April responded. "We're doing a family only dinner tonight in the Spruce Ridge Tavern, then tomorrow we're mostly free until the wedding rehearsal at five o'clock. I was going to ask if you wanted to go for a run with me tomorrow morning? They've got some incredible trails around the resort that I'd love to check out."

One of the things April and I had discovered we had in common was running. She'd joined the track team in high school, but Jack and I were already divorced by then and I was too deep in my addiction to pay attention to my daughter. I'd discovered running during my six-month stay at the treatment center. Running became a good way to push aside the cravings and work through the emotions I used to numb with drugs. To this day, I ran at least five times a week.

"I'd love to go for a run," I told April with a smile. "How about eight o'clock?"

"Awesome. We're going to go to our room and rest a while before dinner. We got one of the suites in the Main Lodge and it's just beautiful. Where are you staying?"

"I'm in the Ridgeview Cabin," I said, pointing at the path. "I think it's just up here."

"Great. You get your bath, and we'll see you at the restaurant tonight at six o'clock."

"Sounds good."

I headed up the path and found my cabin, surprised by how nice it was. It looked like a rustic log cabin from the outside, but the inside was surprisingly modern. It was all dark wood and bright colors, with high end fixtures and expensive looking furniture. It was much nicer than I'd expected, especially because the cabin was cheaper than the suites in the lodge. It had a giant king sized bed with tons of pillows, a seating area with a couch and two chairs, a mini fridge and microwave, a private patio, and a bathroom with a huge jacuzzi tub. I was in heaven.

A couple of hours later I was ready to head to dinner. I'd taken a long hot bath to relax my muscles after the long drive and my run-in with Mr. "I'm Too Important to Look Where I'm Driving", then did a bit of yoga, followed by a nice long meditation to center myself. I was feeling better mentally and physically by the time I was done.

I pulled on a black sundress that was covered with a pattern of little red cherries. I'd bought it especially for this trip. It was comfortable and whimsical, and I loved it. I paired it with sandals and stuffed a shrug in my purse in case I got cold. After blowing out my hair and adding a little make-up, I was ready to see the family.

April waved me over as soon as I stepped inside the restaurant. Bless her, she'd saved me a seat between her and a woman who I assumed was Jonathon's mother. I'd never met her, but I could definitely see the family resemblance.

Jack, my ex-husband, rose from the table and pulled me into a long hug. It was familiar and comforting to be in his arms.

"You look great Kiki," he said, using the nickname he'd made up for me way back when we were first dating.

We pulled apart and I greeted his current wife, Suzanne—the woman who'd raised my daughter through her difficult teenage years after I'd abandoned her. I'd made amends to all of them years ago, and both Jack and Suzanne had been nothing but accepting of me, but I still felt a sharp stab of guilt whenever I was with my ex-husband and his wife.

I slid into the chair next to my daughter and introduced myself to Renee, Jonathon's mother. I knew that Jonathon's father had died many years ago, leaving Renee to raise her kids on her own, although her brother Reed had apparently been very involved.

I felt someone watching me and looked across the table. To my shock, I saw the man who almost ran me over earlier. My mouth dropped open.

"You!" I gasped before I could think better of it.

"Do you two know each other?" Renee asked curiously.

I looked around, not wanting to out him to his family or upset April by causing a scene.

"No," I responded. "We just, um, ran into each other earlier, but we didn't get a chance to introduce ourselves."

A corner of Reed's mouth lifted in a sardonic smile as Jonathon made introductions.

"Erika, this is my uncle, Reed. Reed, this is April's mom, Erika."

"Nice to meet you," I murmured politely.

I was having difficulty pulling my eyes away from his. I felt this weird connection between us, and I had the strangest urge to spend the night staring into his beautiful brown eyes. He really was quite attractive. Breaking the connection, I turned my attention to my daughter, where it belonged.

"What's good here?"

Reed

I can't say I was surprised to run into my mystery woman from earlier. This was a large resort, but somehow I'd known we'd see each other again. I just didn't know she'd be part of the wedding. I wasn't sad about that though. We'd be around each other all weekend and that would make it way easier to get to know her.

I mentally ran through what I knew about April's mother. Jonathon had told me that she lived in New York City, the same as me. He'd mentioned that she and April had been estranged for many years after her parents divorced. I didn't recall hearing what had happened to cause the estrangement.

I appreciated that she didn't tell everyone at the table about our little run-in earlier. I was still embarrassed about it.

Erika looked beautiful tonight. She was wearing a cute dress with cherries on it, and her long brown hair was styled around her face. She looked soft and feminine and when our eyes met earlier, my cock had twitched in interest.

I watched her as we waited for our dinners to arrive. She ordered a soda water, ignoring the wine bottle that was passed around the table, and chatted with my sister Renee. Every so often, Erika glanced at me from the corner of her eye.

My sister caught me staring at Erika and raised an eyebrow at me curiously, but I ignored her.

It was a fairly small group: the bride and groom, my sister, my nephew Mark and his girlfriend, my niece Tammy, April's father Jack and his wife, plus Erika, and myself. I was pleased to see that Erika seemed to have a cordial relationship with her ex-husband and his wife. I knew that wasn't often the case.

We ordered dinner, chatting while we all ate. Well, most of us were chatting. Erika was mostly quiet unless someone asked her a direct question. I wondered if she was shy or uncomfortable or both.

The restaurant was known for its locally sourced grass-fed beef, and we all ordered different cuts of steak or thick juicy burgers. Except for Erika. She ordered some kind of large salad with grilled chicken on it, carefully slicing it up and eating in small, deliberate bites.

Feeling me watching her, she glanced up and I met her gaze. Her eyes widened slightly as we stared at each other, the rest of the room falling away. Erika looked a little confused, and I wondered if it was because she was reacting to the strong pull between us the same way I was. I'd never felt anything like this before, surely I couldn't be alone in how I was feeling?

I heard a chuckle and finally looked away. Renee, April, and Jonathon were all watching us, their gazes speculative. Thankfully, the waitress came to take the plates away, pulling the attention away from us.

When dinner was over, Jack and his wife got up to leave, and my sister did as well, saying she was tired and wanted to go back to her room.

"We're leaving too," Mark told us. His girlfriend and sister Tammy pushed away from the table with him. "We'll be in Franny's Barn if anyone wants to join us."

Seeing our confusion, he added, "It's where the dancing is. April, Jonathon, you should join us later."

Erika set her napkin down on the table. "I should go back to my cabin."

"Please stay for a while, Mom," April asked.

Erika lowered back into the chair as the others walked away, leaving the two of us alone with her daughter and my nephew.

"So Reed," April started, "You and my mom probably have a lot in common."

Erika looked skeptical but didn't say anything.

"What kind of work do you do, Erika?" I asked.

She paused. I'd noticed that she seemed to take a moment to think before she talked.

"I'm a certified alcohol and drug counselor," she replied. "And you?"

"I work in finance."

Erika gave me a long look but didn't add anything. To be fair, a lot of people's eyes glazed over when they heard that I worked with money.

"You're both native New Yorkers, and you both are runners," April announced. "Mom did the New York City Marathon last year."

I was impressed.

"You got in? That's so cool. I've heard it's tough to get accepted."

The race was notoriously hard to get into. So many people wanted to run it there was a lottery or minimum qualifying times for entry.

Another pause.

"It helped that I turned fifty last year, so the qualifying times were lower. It was my first full marathon. I usually stick with half marathons, but I wanted to try my hand at a longer race. It was a great experience."

That was the longest she'd spoken since she sat down at the table, and the most animated that I'd seen her – other than when she was cussing me out earlier. We continued talking for a while, with April and Jonathon prompting conversation when there was a lull. I had the distinct impression that the two of them were trying hard to keep us talking. Suddenly, April made a show of yawning loudly.

"I'd better go get some sleep. Reed, can you walk my mom back to her cabin?"

My nephew's fiancée had a mischievous look on her face that told me she'd noticed the vibes between us and wanted to do a little matchmaking. Plus, I was pretty sure that she and Jonathon were planning on joining Jonathon's siblings at the dance hall.

"That's not necessary," Erika protested. "The resort is very safe, and besides, I have mace in my purse."

"I'd be glad to walk you back," I interrupted. "I'm staying in the cabins too."

Seeing she was outmaneuvered, Erika stood up and gave the kids a hug. I stood up and offered her my arm, but she ignored it, striding out of the restaurant and leaving me to follow. I moved ahead of her, opening the door and forcing her to duck under my arm to get through. I smelled the scent of lavender from her shampoo.

"Which cabin are you in?" I asked.

"Ridgeview," she answered. "It's this way."

"You're in the same section as me," I noted. "I'm in the Forestview cabin."

She didn't respond. We walked for a few minutes before I broke the silence.

"Thanks for not telling both of our families that I tried to run you over," I told her. "How are you feeling?"

"I'm okay, just bruised. I took a hot bath and did some meditation, and that helped relieve the soreness."

"Meditation?" I asked curiously.

"It helps me manage pain. Or stress. Or life, really."

"Ibuprofen works too," I joked.

"I don't take pain killers. I'm in recovery."

She said it in a very matter of fact tone. My mind raced with questions that I didn't know her well enough to ask yet. I wondered if that was the reason she'd been estranged from Jack and April for so long.

"Well, I feel terrible about what happened. Please let me know if there's anything you need."

She didn't answer, and we lapsed into silence again as we walked across the dimly lit path towards our cabins. It was a warm night, and I could hear crickets chirping as we walked through the old growth trees. It felt like we were a million miles away from the hustle and bustle of the city.

"This is me," she said. "Thanks for walking me back."

I followed her right to the door and she visibly stiffened. Scanning the key card, she opened the door slightly, propping it open with her foot, and turned back to face me.

"What are you doing?" she asked, looking up at me. She was tall for a woman, probably about five foot nine, but I still had several inches on her.

"This."

I moved forward slowly, slowly enough for her to push me away, and when she didn't, I pressed my lips against hers. Bringing one hand up to cup the back of her head, I licked along the seam of her lips until she opened for me. The minute our tongues touched, my entire body was on fire. A rush of excitement moved through me, stronger than I'd ever felt in my life.

Mine. The word kept repeating in my mind as I moved closer to her and deepened the kiss. I shoved her against the door, but suddenly, Erika went flying through the doorway and into the cabin. I grabbed the door frame to keep from falling on top of her. Damn it, I'd forgotten she was propping the door open with her foot, and when I pressed my weight against her, the door opened behind her.

She looked up at me from where she was sprawled on the floor, a look of bemusement on her face. Her skirt had ridden high on her shapely legs, and my already erect cock pressed painfully against my zipper.

"Are you an assassin sent to kill me?" she joked.

"I'm so sorry," I said, repeating my words from earlier. "Are you hurt?"

"Just my pride."

I pulled out a hand and helped her stand. She tried to tug her hand away, but I didn't want to let her go. Not now, not when I'd finally found my soulmate after all these years. I was normally a very practical man. I'd never been married, never believed in love at first sight or soulmates, and I'd always assumed I'd be a lifelong bachelor. But all that had changed the moment our eyes had met through my car windshield.

Erika tugged her hand again and I reluctantly released her.

"Look Reed, I'm sure you're a nice guy, despite your strong desire to injure me, and I won't deny that I find you incredibly attractive, but I'm not looking for a vacation fling. I'm here for my daughter, and I'm not going to do anything to make her uncomfortable or take my attention away from her. My relationship with her is too important."

I knew there was more to this story, but I was smart enough not to press my luck.

"I understand. For the record, I'm not looking for a fling either. I want it all. But I'll give you some time to get used to the idea."

I walked back through the door and rapped it with my knuckles. "Be sure to bolt the door. I'll see you tomorrow Erika."

Erika

Reed walked away and I went through the motions of getting ready for bed, my mind racing. That kiss. My God, I'd never felt anything like it. I'd been in love a couple of times, but it had never felt like this before. I'd just met the man. He was my future son-in-law's uncle, and he'd knocked me over twice now, so I should stay far away from him. Yet I felt this strange kind of pull towards him that I couldn't explain.

And what did he mean by 'I want it all'?

You're here for April, I reminded myself. *Nothing else matters.*

I'd been in recovery for five years before I reached out to my daughter and ex-husband to make amends. I wanted to have my five year pin before I told them I was sober. I wanted them to be able to trust that I had changed when I asked to be let back into their lives.

After my divorce I'd completely abandoned my daughter, refusing to show up for even one of our scheduled visitations. Angry about the divorce and in denial about my addiction, I'd bounced around from place to place, job to job, eventually winding up homeless and unemployed. I traded anything I could for oxycodone and alcohol, stealing when I had to.

By some miracle I'd avoided getting hooked on the stronger drugs that were so common on the streets. I'd been hanging out at a drop-in center that offered free lunch to the homeless when I met a woman named Tina. She said she was a peer mentor, someone who'd been an addict like me but had gotten clean. She said she could help me.

"I'm not an addict," I'd protested.

Tina hadn't argued. She'd just patted my arm. "I'm here when you're ready."

A few months later, I was ready. The night before I'd been jumped while sleeping in the park. I'd gotten away, but not before getting beat up pretty badly. It had been the wake-up call I needed. I didn't want to die on the streets, too high to realize what was going on.

I went to see Tina at the drop-in center the very next morning, and by the next day I was enrolled in a treatment program. I found out later that Tina had pulled strings to get me into a program so quickly, and to get me on Medicaid to pay for it.

After six months in treatment, I'd gone to a sort of halfway house for people in recovery. I'd stayed there for a year, getting a job at a local restaurant, and studying to become a peer mentor like Tina. I started working at the same drop-in center where I'd made the decision to get clean and studied for my CADC – the certified alcohol and drug counselor certification.

After doing my required training hours, I'd moved onto a counseling role at a local drug treatment program. I loved my job, and I loved giving back to people who had the same struggles as me. I thanked God every day that Tina had cared enough to help me.

I'd worked hard to make a good life for myself. I had a small but nice apartment, a job I loved, hobbies that I enjoyed, and a small circle of good friends. But I'd missed having family.

When I made contact with Jack and April, I'd expected them to be skeptical. I'd hurt them both, and I'd been a shitty mother to April, too focused on getting high to take care of her properly. I'd reached out to Jack first, meeting him for coffee one afternoon. He'd been nicer than I deserved after all I'd put him through, thrilled to hear that I'd maintained sobriety for so long. He'd promised to share my number with April and let her know I wanted to talk to her.

When April called me the very next day, I'd burst into grateful tears.

Slowly we'd rebuilt our relationship. I'd proudly showed her my five-year sobriety pin and CADC certification and acknowledged the harm that I'd caused her. She'd been tentative at first, and rightly so, but we soon bonded over a shared love of running and horror movies. We'd made an effort to talk a couple of times a month, and periodically get together for dinner, a movie, or a run in Central Park. When things got serious with Jonathon, she'd even brought him to meet me one night over dinner.

Even still, I'd been surprised that she wanted to include me in her wedding celebration. I knew that April had forgiven me, but on some level I didn't trust it yet. I didn't want to rock the boat by making her upset this weekend. My relationship with her was too important.

That's why I was resolved to stay away from Reed and his magic lips. I was too old and way too practical to indulge in a silly crush. It was too bad though. That had been the most amazing first kiss I'd ever had. I'd been dying to invite him into my cabin for more.

I met April in the parking lot the next morning for our run. It was supposed to be a hot day, and we were both dressed in running shorts and tank tops to stay cool. Running in the woods was a nice change from the hard asphalt I usually ran on in the city. The trails were soft and well groomed, and wide enough for us to run side by side and talk.

We were about a mile in when April brought up her fiancé's uncle.

"You and Reed seemed to have some major vibes," she said with a slight teasing quality to her voice.

"There are no vibes," I protested. "I'm one hundred percent focused on you this weekend, April. I want your wedding to be perfect. I promise I won't do anything to mess it up."

My daughter was silent for a long moment.

"Mom, I've forgiven you for what happened when I was a kid. You don't have to walk on eggshells around me. I don't know if I ever told you, but I went to counseling for several years when I was in college. It was helpful. My therapist helped me to understand that addiction is a disease."

She stopped as a family came towards us from the other direction, then picked up the conversation after they passed.

"I've also read about how aggressively doctors and pharmaceutical companies used to push opioids, and how addicting they are. You're not the only person who got hooked on them. You don't have to feel like you need to prove yourself over and over. You and I are good, and if you like Reed, you should go for it. He's been alone for a long time, and so have you. If you guys get together, Jonathon and I will support you one hundred percent. We all will.

"Thanks honey, I appreciate that and I'm so thankful that we have a relationship now. But I'm totally fine alone."

She sent me an appraising look.

"Just because you messed up with Dad, that doesn't mean you have to live like a monk."

"I don't," I protested. I was surprised how well my daughter seemed to understand me.

"When's the last time you dated anyone?" she asked. "You haven't mentioned anyone since we started talking again and that's already been, what? Three years now?"

"It's been a while since I dated anyone," I hedged.

I actually hadn't done more than go on a couple of dates since I got out of treatment. I'd been celibate for so long I was pretty sure I'd regained my virginity. Not that I would share all that with my daughter. We were getting closer, but not that close.

"Just think about it Mom. I want you to be happy. Reed is a great guy, and he seems to really like you."

"I don't need a man to be happy," I protested.

"No, but the right man will help with that."

Reed

"How are you feeling about the big day?"

Jonathon, Mark, and I were golfing along with April's father Jack. There was a golf course not too far from the resort, and it was surprisingly empty for a Saturday morning. Maybe it was because we'd gotten there so early. We were all evenly matched in that each of us liked golf but none of us were particularly good at it.

"I'm feeling great," Jonathon replied. "I can't wait to make April my wife and start a family with her."

Jack slapped him on the back. "We're thrilled you're joining our family."

Jonathon sent me a look.

"Speaking of family, Uncle Reed, what's going on with you and Erika? Did you steal a kiss when you walked her back to her cabin last night?"

I felt my face heat and was glad for my beard to hide it. I was a little too old to be blushing like a schoolgirl.

"Nothing's going on."

"But you like her?" Jonathon pressed.

"Yeah, I do."

"You should ask her out. She can be your date for the wedding," Mark suggested.

"She's a great woman," Jack added. "She's had a rough life. She had a shitty childhood and things were pretty bad when we got divorced, but she's really changed her life since then."

"I, um, suggested that we spend more time together," I admitted, not sharing that we'd kissed. "But she turned me down. She says she doesn't want to upset April."

"April would be thrilled if you guys got together," Jonathon told me. "We were talking about it last night. We think you're perfect for each other."

"Well, we'll need to convince her of that."

Jonathon took out his phone and started texting furiously. I shook my head. These kids were always on their phones.

We turned in our loaner golf clubs and headed back to the resort. As we exited the parking lot and walked along the edge of the wooded area, someone suddenly ran out from the trail. It was Erika and April coming back from their run. They were dressed almost identically in shorts and tanks, looking so much alike no one would doubt that they were mother and daughter.

My eyes trailed appreciatively over the long length of Erika's toned legs, before checking out the soft swell of her breasts beneath her tank. With her hair pulled back in a ponytail, she didn't look too much older than April.

"Hey sweetie!" April trilled, rushing over to greet Jonathon. He tried to hug her, but she stepped back. "I'm all sweaty. Mom put me through my paces."

Erika smiled. "I'm sweaty too. It's hot outside."

I stepped closer to Erika, like a moth drawn to a flame. "Good morning. How was your run?"

Her face was impassive, but her eyes looked wary.

"It was great, thank you."

She called to her daughter, "I'm going to head back to my cabin. Let me know if you need anything."

"Okay Mom, thanks. I will," April responded. "Thanks for the run, it was great."

"I'll walk with you," I told Erika, pointing towards the path that led to the cabin area.

She opened her mouth to object, and I reminded her, "My cabin is close to yours."

Jonathon gave me a 'thumbs up' behind Erika's back and mouthed, "Good luck."

"What are your plans for today?" I asked Erika as we headed towards our section of cabins.

There was a slight pause as she chose her words.

"Take a shower. Then I'm going to grab some lunch and check out the pool."

"May I join you?"

"I don't know you well enough to shower with you," she teased with a tiny smile.

"We'll save that for tomorrow then," I teased back. "Can I buy you lunch? I owe you after the way I hit you with my car. And pushed you through a door."

She rolled her eyes. "Fine. How about we meet at the dining room in an hour? I heard they have outdoor seating, and I wouldn't mind getting some sunshine."

I started to tell her that I'd pick her up but decided not to press my luck.

"See you then."

I was waiting at a table on the veranda when Erika came in, dressed in a dark red bathing suit, one of those flowered skirts women liked to wear over bathing suits, flip flops, and a big, floppy straw sunhat. She looked beautiful.

I waived to get her attention, and she made her way over to me. Our eyes met and held until she bumped into a chair, knocking it over and almost falling on top of someone's table before stopping herself with her hand. I rushed over as she righted the chair and apologized to the people at the table.

"I'm starting to think you're accident prone," I said, taking her elbow to lead her back to the table. My fingers burned where I touched her.

"I'm starting to think you're bad luck," she rejoined.

She took off her hat as we sat down, shaking out her hair, then looked down at her menu. The waitress hurried over with coffee. Erika took a long drink, her eyes closing in pleasure. I noticed she drank it black, same as me.

"Do you know what you want to eat?" the young waitress asked, looking at Erika.

"I'll take an order of scrambled eggs and a bowl of fresh fruit please, with a cup of cottage cheese if you have it."

"Toast? Bacon? Sausage?" the waitress asked.

"No thank you."

I ordered an omelet with bacon and toast. When the waitress left, I looked at my companion.

"How'd you get into running?" I asked.

"I started running when I was in treatment," she said after a slight pause. "It was a good way to take my mind off...everything and lose some weight."

"You don't need to lose weight," I told her, my eyes falling to her shapely breasts before snapping back up.

"I did then," she said quietly. "I was at least fifty pounds heavier when I went into treatment, plus it's pretty common to gain weight in the early days of recovery. How about you? Do you do a lot of running?"

I had the distinct sense that she wasn't comfortable talking about herself.

"Yeah, I started years ago. My job is pretty demanding, and the good thing about running is you can do it any time and you don't have to buy a bunch of equipment."

"Except good running shoes," she said. "Do you run races?"

I shook my head. "I've never done a race, but I religiously run three to five miles most days unless I'm doing something else active." I patted my still-flat stomach. "Like you said, it's a good way to burn calories, and I don't want to let myself go."

"You don't need to lose weight," she repeated my words from earlier and I gave her a smile.

Conversation flowed between us more easily than I expected. After talking about running and hobbies, we asked each other about our jobs. It was clear that Erika loved her job and got a sense of purpose from it, more than I got from mine, that was for sure. I liked it, was good at it, and made an obscene amount of money, most of which I'd invested to make even more money. But money wasn't everything.

After lunch we headed over to the pool. After getting beach towels from the attendant, we spread out on side by side chaise loungers. Erika removed her skirt thing, and I checked out her slim body out of the corner of my eye. Her ass was a work of art – round but muscled. I had an image of pounding into her from behind, my hands gripping those cheeks, and pulled off my shirt and spread it across my lap just in case. I was already half hard and this was a family resort.

Erika turned, giving my naked chest an appreciative look. Her eyes turned dark, and she licked her lips before she caught herself and turned away. We lay side-by-side, lost in our thoughts, until my family caught up with us.

Erika

The warm sun had almost lulled me to sleep when I heard someone calling our names. Sitting up, I saw April coming towards us with Jonathon and Renee in tow. Renee settled into the chair on my opposite side, leaning back with a contented sigh. Meanwhile April and Jonathon pulled off their clothes, piling them up next to us, and headed into the pool for a dip.

After a few minutes of silence Renee called across me to Reed.

"How's everything going big brother?" she asked in a singsong tone.

Reed turned his head and gave his sister a look that was almost suspicious.

"Fine. You?"

Renee's sharp eyes moved between us, but she didn't say anything. I wondered if she thought it was weird that we were together.

"Your brother bought me lunch, so I didn't have to eat alone, and then we decided to sunbathe," I rushed to say, as if I needed to explain why we were together by the pool.

Renee's eyes went to my thigh, where a nice bruise had formed just beneath the line of my bathing suit.

"What happened?" she asked, pointing at the bruise.

I glanced at Reed. "Umm..."

Renee laughed. "Oh, never mind, I don't want to know."

I looked at her in confusion. "Huh?"

"The last thing I want to hear about is my brother's sex life."

My face was instantly red. "Oh, no, we're not, I mean, we never, it's not..."

Reed interrupted, saving me from my stammering.

"It's from when I hit her with my car yesterday."

"What?!?!"

30

Renee's voice was shocked. Just then April and Jonathon returned, catching the tail end of our conversation.

"You're the one who almost ran her over?" April asked, toweling off her long hair as her gaze switched back and forth between us.

"I would say that was a romcom meet-cute if my poor mom hadn't gotten banged up."

"It was an accident," I protested. "I'm fine."

I don't know why I was defending him, but I hated to see him be embarrassed in front of his family. Plus, the last thing I wanted was for April to worry about me when she should be focusing on her wedding.

"I wasn't looking where I was going," Reed added. "I saw a spot and swerved into it at the last minute. Fortunately, Erika thought quickly and jumped on my hood before I crushed her."

"Way to make a good first impression, Uncle Reed." Jonathon's voice was teasing.

All the attention was making me uncomfortable. I didn't want to make a spectacle of myself or add any stress to April's wedding weekend. I sat up and rooted around for my sarong.

"I'm getting hot. I think I'll go back to my room for a while."

I stood up, wrapping the sarong around my waist. Out of the corner of my eye, I could see Reed staring at me appreciatively. I ignored him, although my nipples took notice, hardening against the fabric of my swimsuit. I hunched my shoulders and sent my daughter a smile.

"I'll see you at the rehearsal."

Reed jumped out of his chair with the athleticism of a much younger man.

"Let me walk with you."

"No, I'm fine." I waved him away. "You hang out and enjoy the sun."

He sat back down reluctantly. "Okay, we'll see you later."

I headed back to my room to do some yoga and meditate. I'd just finished a meditation session on my veranda when my phone rang.

"Mom? I need a favor."

"Anything," I answered quickly.

"I just realized that I forgot my lipstick for the wedding tomorrow," April said.

"Oh no."

"I was planning to wear the Sephora brand vegan lipstick, the hibiscus one," she continued, talking quickly. "Would you mind going into town to grab one for me? There's a mall about half an hour from here. I would go but Jonathon and I need to meet with the wedding planner in a few minutes."

"No problem, I can go."

I felt the weirdest rush of pleasure that my daughter was depending on me to do something, even if it was just picking up a lipstick.

"Great, thanks so much Mom. I'll text you the shade, so you remember. Oh, and Reed will be by to pick you up in a few minutes."

"What? I don't need a ride, I have my car here," I protested.

"Reed knows where the mall is."

"I have GPS."

"I just talked to him, and he says he doesn't mind going with you. Thanks Mom, I really appreciate this."

April ended the call, and I couldn't help but wonder if this was all a set-up. Was my daughter playing matchmaker? Or did she think I really couldn't find my way to the store and pick out a lipstick?

Before I could decide, there was a knock on the door. I sighed as I went to let Reed in. He'd changed since I last saw him, putting on khaki shorts, running shoes, and a navy t-shirt that hugged his impressive chest. A pair of sunglasses was tucked into the neckline. He looked like a cologne commercial.

"Let me just grab my purse," I told him as I walked back into the cabin.

Reed grabbed my hand, pulling me back towards him.

"What are you doing?" I asked.

"What I've been dying to do all day."

Before I could respond, he lowered his lips to mine. The instant we touched, my entire body was on fire. Forgetting my resolve to keep my distance, I wrapped my hands around his neck, stepping closer, and opened my mouth for his probing tongue. He swept in, his tongue tangling with mine as the kiss went on and on. When we finally came up for breath, my panties were damp, my heart was racing, and I'd forgotten all about April's lipstick.

"As much as I'd like to continue this, we'd better get to the mall," he said.

I felt a stab of disappointment, even as I reminded myself that I was here for April, not to have a torrid affair with her fiancé's silver fox uncle. I looked around for my purse and my phone, then joined Reed at the door.

"Let's go."

I followed him to the parking lot, slipping into the passenger seat of his black Mercedes.

"Nice ride," I said.

It was much nicer than my fifteen-year-old Corolla, although that car was paid off and ran like a dream, so I had no complaints.

"I really would have been fine by myself," I told him as he backed out of the parking spot.

Reed spared me a glance. "I got the sense April really wanted me to go with you," he replied.

"Clearly."

"Well partner, let's head to the mall and save this wedding."

Reed

Erika was mostly quiet as we drove to the mall, but I'd already seen that she wasn't much of a talker. It was a pleasant change from the women I usually dated, who tended to jabber on and fill any silence.

I focused on the road as I replayed that kiss in my head about a hundred times. I'd never felt such an intense attraction to someone before. It would be scary if it didn't feel so right.

We got to the mall, and I started looking for a parking spot. Like every mall in America, it was a huge, sprawling building surrounded by about a million parking spots, none of which were free.

"Try not to run anyone over," Erika teased, breaking her long silence as I finally found a spot after several minutes of circling around.

"Har har, very funny," I said as I carefully parked in an open spot.

We headed into the mall, checking out the sign to figure out where Sephora was. After locating the store on the map, we walked in companionable silence, both of us people watching in the crowded mall. It was Labor Day weekend, and the weather was beautiful, yet half the people in Virginia were at this mall it seemed.

"This is the place," Erika said, stopping in front of a store halfway across the mall.

I followed her inside, looking around. "There's a whole store just for make-up?" I asked incredulously.

"No, they sell hair products and lotion here too."

I laughed. I was the only man in the store and received a few weird looks as I followed Erika to one of the many lipstick displays.

"What are we looking for?" I asked as I looked around.

"Hibiscus lipstick."

"Is it flavored lipstick?" I asked.

Erika giggled. "No, that's the name of the lipstick shade. It'll be a dark pink, like hibiscus flowers."

"Like this?" I asked a few minutes later, holding up a tube of lipstick that looked dark pink.

"No, that's coral."

She turned the tube over, her small hand brushing against mine. "See? The color is printed on the bottom, and this one says coral."

I shook my head. "You women have way more colors than men do."

She didn't answer, focused on scanning the lipsticks. She held one up triumphantly. "Vegan hibiscus. Yay!"

"I thought hibiscus was a flower," I asked in confusion.

"It is."

"So wouldn't all hibiscus be vegan then?"

Erika laughed, a wide smile lighting up her face, and I forgot how to breathe. I'd never seen anything other than the reserved half smile she offered everyone. It felt like a gift to see a real smile on her beautiful face, even if it was at my expense.

"No, the lipstick is vegan, not the hibiscus. Well hibiscus is vegan too but there's not any actual hibiscus in the lipstick."

I shook my head. "If you say so."

We walked towards the cash register, waiting for our turn to check out. I gaped when I heard the price but resisted saying anything. Who knew that a tiny tube of lipstick would be so expensive? After paying, Erika slipped the precious lipstick into her purse, and we headed back to the car.

As we pulled out, I noticed an ice cream stand across the street from the mall, the sign advertising soft serve.

"Ooh! I haven't had soft serve in years. Do you mind if we stop? Ice cream would hit the spot."

"I love soft serve," she replied. "I don't think I've had it since April was a baby."

I parked near the stand and we both ordered cones. Erika ordered vanilla with a chocolate dip, while I got the chocolate with rainbow sprinkles. We scoped out a nearby bench and sat side by side eating our cones.

"This is delicious," she said. "I almost never eat ice cream. I'd forgotten how good it is."

I glanced over at Erika, noting that she had a smear of ice cream on the corner of her lip. I reached over and scooped it up with my finger, then licked it off. Erika's eyes widened as she watched me.

I can't say who moved first, but suddenly we flew towards each other, dropping the rest of our cones on the ground as we met in a flurry of lips and hands. I lifted Erika by the waist, pulling her to straddle me as the kiss went on and on. Erika ground her hips against my painfully hard cock, and I moaned against her mouth.

Suddenly a sharp voice came from behind us. "This is a family place. Get a room!"

Erika jumped at the sound of the judgmental voice and somehow managed to fall off my lap, landing on the ground with a squeak of surprise. I sent up a prayer of thanks that we'd chosen a bench in the grass and not one of the benches that ran along the sidewalk.

"Are you okay?" I asked as I reached for her hand to help her up. "Did you hurt yourself?"

"You wouldn't need to keep asking me that if you weren't very obviously trying to kill me," she said wryly.

I met her gaze. "There are many things I want to do to you Erika, but killing you is not on the list. Besides, that one wasn't my fault."

She stood up, brushing off her shorts with a grimace. "If I keep hanging around with you, I'm going to be one big bruise by the time I leave on Monday."

I threw my arm around her shoulders and squeezed her close to me as we walked back to the car. I felt ridiculously happy when she didn't pull away.

"Maybe we should stop at the hardware store and get you some bubble wrap while we're here," I teased.

"Haha. You're a funny guy."

"Speaking of hanging around with me, will you be my date for the rehearsal dinner?"

She looked up at me with her brow crinkled in confusion.

"We're both going to be there anyway, we don't need dates. And while I appreciate the offer, I really need to keep my focus on April this weekend."

"In case you haven't noticed, April is part of the plot to fix us up. Do you really think she needed a lipstick that much?"

"You think it was all a ruse?"

"I'm betting it was. Someone's coming to do her hair and make-up before the wedding, right? I heard her and Renee talking about it. Wouldn't the make-up person bring their own supplies?"

"Well crap, I think you're right."

I opened the passenger door and waited for her to get inside before I went around to the driver's side.

"Do you still think April will be upset if we're together?" I asked.

Erika looked over at me, her expression troubled.

"Look Reed, even if April is okay with it, I don't want to be distracted from the wedding. I've let my daughter down her whole life, I'm not going to risk not being available when she needs me."

"What about when we get back to New York?"

She shook her head before I even finished my sentence.

"I don't have time to date, sorry. Besides, with our family connections, it could get messy."

I decided to put all my cards on the table.

"Something big is happening here," I told her, my voice husky. "I've never felt like this before Erika."

"Neither have I," she admitted. "But we'll get over it."

"I don't think we will," I answered. "But I won't push you. Yet. I can see you're scared."

Her eyes widened in surprise, telling me that my guess was right.

"But I won't quit trying," I warned her. "Especially now that I know I'm not the only one feeling this way."

"Let's just get back to the resort," she whispered. "April might need me."

Erika

By the time we got back to Mountain Ridge Resort, it was almost time for the rehearsal. I changed into a colorful peasant skirt and a white off the shoulder top, pairing it with the same sandals I'd worn last night. That was the beauty of black shoes, you could match them to almost anything.

I heard a knock on the door and wasn't surprised to find Reed on the other side. He was nothing if not persistent.

"Did you come to knock me down again?"

I couldn't resist teasing him. I was usually pretty serious, but something about Reed seemed to bring out my whimsical side.

He looked incredibly handsome in black dress pants and a lightweight white dress shirt that was open at the neck. His hair was slightly damp at the ends, and I caught a tantalizing whiff of aftershave.

"Shall we?" he asked, offering me his arm.

I was tempted to remind him that I'd declined his offer to be his date for the rehearsal, but it felt churlish, so I kept my mouth shut and wrapped my hand through the crook of his arm. Like every time we touched, I felt sparks of electricity where my hand met his skin.

Neither of us had a role in the actual wedding, so we settled down in the back of the chapel where the wedding would take place, watching the kids practice while the wedding planner barked orders like a drill sergeant.

"She's good," I whispered as she quieted a couple of joking groomsmen with just a stern look.

I felt myself tear up as I watched Jack walk April down the aisle, the way he would tomorrow. All those years we were estranged, I thought I'd never see my daughter again. To be here, included in her wedding even after everything that had happened, it meant everything to me.

I sniffed quietly, and Reed hooked his arm over my shoulders, pulling me close. I leaned into his warmth and watched as Jack mimed handing April over to her groom. She stepped towards the alter and caught her sandal on the edge of the step. We all watched in horror as she flew forward, knocking the Reverend back several steps as she crashed into him, then landed on her knees.

Jonathon rushed over to help her up.

"I'm fine," she called to everyone as she popped to her feet with the agility of the young. "Nothing is hurt, except for my pride."

"Like mother like daughter," Reed whispered in my ear.

I playfully smacked his chest. "Shush."

After the rehearsal was finished, we headed to the small banquet room that the kids had reserved for the rehearsal dinner. This was a bigger group than we had last night, with the addition of the wedding party and a few other close friends of April and Jonathon's. We were separated into several large round tables and somehow I ended up sitting between my ex-husband and Reed, with Suzanne on the other side of Jack.

"How are you doing there, Mom?" Jack asked me facetiously.

"I'm going to need to bring a box of Kleenex tomorrow," I confided to my ex. "Just watching the rehearsal made me emotional. I don't know how I'm going to get through the actual wedding."

He leaned closer with a wry smile. "Me too. I'm going to be a blubbering mess tomorrow."

Dinner wrapped up, and the young people were making plans to go dancing. Apparently they'd all had a wild time at Franny's Barn last night.

With the party breaking up, the rest of our table was milling around the room. Reed left to use the restroom and Jack leaned towards me with a twinkle in his eyes.

"So, you and Reed, huh?"

I shook my head. "Oh no. He's just being nice since I'm here alone."

"Really? It seems like you two have some serious sparks."

I met my ex-husband's eye. "You know better than anyone how terrible I am at relationships, Jack. I'm much better off alone."

He shot a look at his wife, having one of those silent conversations that couples could have, and Suzanne left the table without a word, leaving us alone to talk.

"You only sucked in relationships after your addiction took hold. I remember how you were before the car accident, before the drugs and the drinking, back when you were a doting wife and mother. The way you made me a lunch every night to take with me to work, the way you spent hours at the dining room table trying to teach April to read before we realized that she was dyslexic."

He tapped his chest.

"I know how good your heart is Kiki. And I've seen how far you've come since you've been in recovery. It's been eight years, don't you think it's time to do something for yourself? Reed's a great guy. He's exactly what I'd want for you. If you like him, you should go for it."

We both stopped talking when Reed came back to the table. He looked between us curiously, sensing the heavy vibe.

"Would you like to take a walk, Erika? The sun will be setting soon, and I've heard the lake is the best place to watch a sunset."

"Sure."

I stood up and Jack did as well, pulling me into a tight hug.

"Take a chance Kiki," he whispered in my ear. "You're strong enough to handle it, no matter what happens."

We went to say goodbye to April and Jonathon, and both my daughter and her fiancé looked as happy to see us leaving together as Jack had. I wondered idly if everyone here was trying to get me and Reed together.

We headed outside, walking slowly as we made our way across the grounds towards the lake area. It was a warm evening, and we didn't pass too many people on the way there despite the fact that the lodge was completely filled for the holiday.

The sky was already turning orange above the trees, signaling that the sun would set soon. The lake was clear and beautiful. It was fed by a freshwater spring, keeping it cold year round, and no motorized vehicles were allowed on the pristine water. We stopped on the shore, sitting on a short dock they used for the paddleboats.

Reed moved behind me, pulling me between his legs and wrapping his arms around my waist. I allowed myself to lean back against his strong chest. We were both lost in thought as we stared out at the water. I replayed my conversation with my ex-husband. Maybe Jack was right. Maybe I could do something for myself – as long as it didn't distract me from my daughter.

I turned to look at Reed as the orange sky turned to red, and the sun dropped past the horizon, making everything instantly darker.

"It's so beautiful."

His expression was serious. "You're so beautiful."

Our eyes met and held.

"I want to kiss you more than I want my next breath," Reed whispered.

"We seem to have bad luck with kissing," I reminded him. "Somehow I always wind up flying through the air when you kiss me. I really don't want to end up in the lake. This is a new outfit, and I heard the water is cold."

"Maybe we need to try kissing in a controlled environment," he teased. "Like my bed."

I made a decision.

"Maybe we do."

His eyes widened. "What are you saying?"

"Take me back to your cabin, Reed. I can't promise you anything beyond tonight, but I want you too."

He surged to his feet and grabbed my hand, pulling me up to standing.

"Let's go."

Reed

I resisted the temptation to throw Erika over my shoulder and carry her back to my cabin. She was thin, maybe thinner than she should be, but we'd had too many near misses. I didn't want to injure her again before we got to the good stuff. Instead, I just got a good grip on her hand and pulled her behind me.

We half jogged back through the dim light towards my cabin. Rushing up the stairs, I slapped the key card against the lock impatiently as I waited for the green light. I was scared to death that Erika would change her mind. The minute the door unlocked I pushed through, spinning Erika around. The door slammed behind us, and I backed her up against it.

"It opens in, don't worry," I joked.

I stepped closer, crowding her, laying gentle kisses along the tops of her shoulders, bared by the design of her shirt. Erika reached up and pulled my head up, meeting my gaze.

"Reed, I haven't had sex in eight years," she said impatiently. "Let's not fuck around."

My dick went from half-mast to a full hard-on in the space of a few seconds.

"Eight years? I'd better make it good then."

"You'd better make it fast then," she said, rolling her hips against mine.

"How about fast first, then slow later?" I negotiated.

"Sounds good."

She slipped under my arms and stalked over to the bed, removing her shirt and strapless bra as she walked. I watched as she shimmied out of her skirt, leaving her just in a pair of skimpy silk panties. She turned to face me, her eyes burning with desire. Her body was long and lean but still softly rounded. She was beautiful.

I unbuttoned my shirt and tossed it over my shoulder.

"Well, look what you're hiding under those fancy shirts," she murmured, admiring my chest.

I loved this playful side of Erika. I had a feeling she didn't let it out very often.

I stalked towards her and gripped my hands on either side of her face. Our kiss was almost frantic. She pulled away and reached for my zipper, opening my pants and shoving them down with my boxers. My cock sprang free, bouncing up to greet her, and Erika wrapped one hand around me. Her soft hand stroked up and down my length, her thumb rubbing against the slit at the end with every stroke.

I'd never wanted a woman as much as I wanted Erika. I know I'd said this would be fast, but if she kept this up I'd come way faster than I wanted. There was no way I was coming before she did.

"On the bed," I growled.

She raised one eyebrow at my aggressive tone but stepped back to sit at the edge of the mattress. I kicked my pants the rest of the way off and dropped to my knees in front of her. I spread her legs, looking at her glistening pussy, and couldn't resist getting a taste. I lifted her legs over my shoulders and lowered my head, giving her a long, slow lick. She tasted as delicious as she looked. I loved giving oral and I was pretty damn good at it. Erika moaned as I repeated the motion.

My lips homed in on her clit, sucking the tiny bundle into my mouth as I slid one finger into her channel. Her hips arched, and I used my other hand to pin her hip to the mattress. I slid my finger in and out, feeling her wetness, and added a second finger, stretching her. I wasn't a small man, and if she'd been celibate for so many years, she likely needed some preparation.

I bent my fingers, searching for her G-spot, and when I found it she came with a long moan. I lifted my head to watch her come apart as I continued moving my fingers deep inside her. Her face was flushed, and her head was moving from side to side while her fingers gripped the bedspread tightly.

She was a vision. I felt a rush of love for her that took my breath away. Suddenly Erika looked up at me.

"I need you inside me," she gasped.

I stiffened. "Oh crap. I just realized I don't have a condom."

She raised her head in exasperation. "You don't have a condom? Doesn't every single guy have a condom?"

I shook my head.

She dropped her head, then raised it again. "I had my tubes tied after April was born. And I haven't had sex in eight years, so I'm clean."

"I haven't been with anyone for over a year," I confessed. "I had a physical a few months ago and everything was clear."

"Bareback it is."

My eyes widened. My entire life I'd never been inside a woman without a condom. I'd never even considered it. But now I wanted nothing more than to make love to Erika without any barriers.

I surged up and Erika slid farther back on the bed. I crawled over her like a predator, my heart pounding so hard I wondered if I'd have a heart attack.

I wedged my hips between her thighs, my cock sliding between her folds, and lowered myself until I could kiss her. Our tongues tangled for a few breaths before Erika pulled back, panting. She lifted her legs, wrapping them around my waist and rolling her hips against mine.

"Now Reed, please."

I pushed inside her with one long push, groaning as I felt her channel hugging my cock tightly. Without the barrier of a condom, everything felt different, more sensitive. Erika made a sound that was halfway between a squeal and a groan.

"Are you okay?"

She nodded. "Yeah, I just need a second to adjust."

She took a deep breath, held it in, then exhaled slowly. I could feel the tight vise of her pussy loosening.

"Okay, go," she ordered.

Bracing myself on my forearms, I started pounding into her, straining to fuck her as deeply as I could, yielding to some primal urge to mark her as mine. There was none of that awkward fumbling that usually happened with a new partner. Our bodies seemed completely in sync.

"Yes!" she hissed, her eyes closing in pleasure.

I pressed my feet against the bottom of the mattress and kept a brutal pace. I couldn't get enough of this woman. I wanted to possess her inside and out. I wanted to come so deep inside her that she'd never forget me. It was ridiculously caveman of me, but I couldn't help it.

Suddenly Erika cried out.

"Ow!"

My head snapped up to see her rubbing the top of her head. A head that was pressed against the headboard. I was pounding into her so hard that I'd shifted us up the mattress with each rough stroke.

"It figures you'd fuck me into a head injury," she joked. "So much for your idea of a controlled environment."

I rolled over, taking her with me.

"Ride me," I ordered. "It's safer that way."

She shifted into a better position, bracing herself on my chest, and began moving herself up and down my cock, twisting her hips on each downward stroke. Her breasts bounced with the effort, mesmerizing me.

My eyes rolled up into the back of my head as I tried to forestall my orgasm. I was close, so close, but I wanted her to come first.

I reached between us and found her clit with my fingers, pinching it lightly, and Erika moaned as another orgasm hit her. She shook on top of me, and I moved my hands to grip her hips, fucking her from below until my own orgasm hit me like a freaking freight train. I pushed up into her, releasing my seed in several long spurts as I groaned her name like a vow.

When I was done, I rolled us over again until we were both resting on our sides, still connected. I couldn't bear to let her go yet.

She gave me a smile.

"I can't believe you rolled us twice without me falling off the bed," she joked. Her breath was still coming in short pants as she tried to catch her breath.

"I figured we'd save that for next time."

We lay there staring at each other for a few minutes before I finally slid away from her, going to the bathroom to clean up. I returned with a cloth, gently wiping away our shared juices from the juncture of her thighs while she watched me in bemused surprise. Tossing the cloth in the direction of the bathroom, I laid back down on the bed next to her. She was laying on her back, and I slid one leg over hers, wrapped my arm around her waist, and rested my head on her chest, just above her left breast.

That's how I fell asleep.

Erika

I woke up with a start. The sun was shining brightly through the windows, the drapes left open. Crap, it was morning. I hadn't intended to stay over. After our first round, Reed and I had snuggled and talked for hours before making love again. I'd fallen into an exhausted sleep afterwards.

I was shocked at how comfortable I'd been talking to him and sleeping with him – actually sleeping I mean. I'd slept alone for many years and even when I was married I'd been disturbed whenever Jack had moved around, and I'd always hated snuggling. But last night I'd slept straight through, content to be wrapped up in Reed's embrace.

I slid out from underneath his arm and headed for the bathroom. I peed, washed my hands, then looked around for my clothes. He was still snoring softly when I was finished. I debated waking him up or leaving a note but decided against it. I was going to see him later anyway, and he'd no doubt figure out that I went back to my place.

I made the short walk back to my cabin, stopping dead when I saw April standing on the porch, her hand raised to knock. She was dressed in running clothes and I had a flash of fear that I'd spaced out on a running date. She turned as I walked up.

"Good morning, Mom." She gave me a teasing smile as she noticed I was wearing the same clothes from last night. "Ah, doing the walk of shame, huh?"

I felt my face heat up.

"I'm sorry." I wasn't totally sure what I was apologizing for, but it seemed like a good start.

"Why are you apologizing?" she laughed. "You're both single, and you already know that we were all hoping that you and Reed would get together. We were all talking about it before we came here, thinking about fixing you up. Then when we saw all the sparks between you two, we knew we were right."

She paused. "You were with Reed, right?"

"Of course," I said defensively. It wasn't like I made a habit of sleeping around with a bunch of strange men. Not that my daughter would know that, I reminded myself.

"Are you up for a run?" she asked. "I know it's early, but I woke up full of nervous energy, so I thought I'd pop over and see if you wanted to come with me."

"That would be great," I responded. "Let me change real quick."

I pulled on my running clothes and followed April towards the woods. We made our way towards the same trail we'd run on yesterday. It was already warm out, despite the fact that it was just after seven in the morning, and the sun beat down on us even through the trees.

April was running a little faster than normal, making me think she had something on her mind. I had a flash of memory of April as a child. Sometimes when she would get upset she would run in circles in the backyard until she got over what was bothering her or was exhausted, whichever came first. Like me, she used exercise as a way to work through her emotions. Or at least that's what I did now that I didn't use drugs to numb my feelings.

"Are you okay?" I asked. "Anything you want to talk about?"

"Am I making a mistake?" My daughter's voice was small and unsure. "Marrying Jonathon, I mean."

Ah yes, I'd suspected this was what she was anxious about. Not that I blamed her; I had been a nervous wreck on my wedding day. My own mother hadn't been the slightest bit interested in allaying my wedding day nerves, but then again she'd never liked Jack anyway.

"How long have you been dating Jonathon?"

"Three years."

"And how long have you been living together?"

"Two years."

"I'm guessing you've had the chance to see him at his best and his worse, right? You know all his annoying habits? How he acts when he's sick or stressed out or drinks too much."

"Yeah, I've seen all that for sure."

"And he's seen the same thing with you, right? He's seen you at your worst? Like when you have cramps or you're cranky from work? He's heard you fart and knows that you poop?"

"Oh yeah," she laughed. "Definitely."

"I'm guessing that you've had some fights over the last three years? Some days when you were tempted to grab a lamp and smash it over his head?"

She nodded.

"Yes, we've had some big blow-ups, but we agreed early on never to go to bed angry with each other, and so far it's worked for us. Not that we fight a lot anyway."

"Knowing all of his faults and bad habits, do you still love him?"

"With all my heart."

"Do you believe he loves you?"

"Without a doubt."

"How do you feel if you think about breaking up with him? How would it be if you never saw him again?"

"That would be devastating. We broke up once for three weeks and it almost killed both of us."

"Knowing all of that, does marrying him feel like a mistake?"

"No."

"Are you sure? Because I've got a car here. We can be gone in ten minutes if you need a getaway ride. You can hide out at my place. I'll even let you have the couch."

She laughed, then came to a stop. I ran a few steps past her before I realized it. April walked closer and pulled me into a sweaty hug.

"Thanks Mom, that really helps."

"I'm glad."

She pulled back and gave me a fond smile that warmed my heart. "I'm so happy you're here."

"Me too honey. I love you, you know."

"Right back at you, Mom."

We started running again, a little slower now, heading back to the lodge area.

"So do you like Reed?" she asked. "I mean, I assume that you do if you spent the whole night with him?"

I decided to be honest.

"I do like him, a lot," I admitted. "But it's just a vacation thing. Things would never work out with us. We're not a good match."

"Why not?"

"He's a rich and successful finance guy, and I'm a formerly homeless drug addict who completely fucked up her first marriage."

April stopped running again and gave me a stern look.

"Mom! You're a successful alcohol and drug counselor and a person who's been through hell and come back stronger. You deserve all the love in the world, and he seems really into you. Jonathon and Renee said they've never seen him so smitten before. Please, don't push Reed away based on superficial differences. If it feels right, if you like him as much as he likes you, then you should go for it. And if Reed's not the right guy for you, find someone else who makes you happy. You deserve that."

"Thanks. That's good advice."

"Of course it is," she said smugly. "Now let's get our heartrates back up and sweat out the rest of my nerves so I'll feel calm when I get married."

Reed

I woke up alone. I wasn't really surprised. Erika had wanted to leave last night, but then I'd distracted her with another round of vigorous love-making. We'd both fallen into an exhausted sleep afterward. It had been heaven sleeping with her wrapped in my arms.

I started to text her, then realized that I didn't have her number. I threw on some clothes and headed over to her cabin. When I came around the corner I ran into Erika and April walking from the opposite direction. They were dressed in running clothes but holding what looked like fruit smoothies, telling me that they must have stopped at the juice bar on their way back from their run.

"Well Reed, what a surprise to see you here," April called, her voice teasing.

"Hey ladies, how was your run?"

"Great," April said. She gave me a knowing look, making me wonder if she knew where her mother had spent the night.

"I'm going to go back to the Main Lodge and see what my fiancé is up to. Mom I'll see you at four for hair and make-up with the rest of the girls."

"Okay honey."

April flitted away and I moved closer to Erika. I grabbed her smoothie and took a sip, then I grimaced, trying not to gag.

"Yuk. What's in this?"

"Wheatgrass."

"Jeez, warn a guy, would you? It tastes like shit."

"That's what you get for stealing a girl's smoothie," she said teasingly.

I breathed a sigh of relief that things didn't feel awkward between us. I'd thought they might.

"I can't believe you went for a run after last night. Aren't you sore?"

She shrugged. "I always feel better after a run. Besides, April needed some girl talk."

"What are you going to do now?"

She gave me a coy look. "Take a shower, then a nap. Do you want to join me?"

"Best idea ever."

***

"Have you ever been married?"

I looked down at Erika who was snuggled against my side. She'd shocked the hell out of me by dropping to her knees in the shower, taking me into her mouth, and sucking me off until I damn near forgot my own name. When she was done I'd dragged her to the bed and returned the favor. With our track record, I didn't want to try any complicated acrobatics in the shower. April would kill me if her mother came to the wedding in a cast.

"No, I've never been married," I responded. "Never even lived with a woman."

"Have you lived with a man?" she teased.

"Nope." I gave her a squeeze. "I never found a man or a woman who I liked enough to make a long term commitment to."

Until now, I added silently. I was so far gone for this woman, I felt like I'd been hit by a train. Last night had just confirmed that she was the woman for me. I only prayed that she felt the same. She was so guarded, it was almost impossible to know what she was thinking.

"Besides, whenever I started getting serious with someone, they would inevitably become upset by how much time I spent at work, and how much time I spent with Renee and the kids."

I understood now why I'd never been able to contemplate making a commitment to another person. I'd blamed work or my family commitments, but in truth none of those other women had been Erika, I just didn't know that's what I was waiting for.

"April told me you stepped in to help after Jonathon's dad died. She said you never missed a sports event or a birthday."

"Yeah I love Jonathon, Terry, and Mark like they're my own kids."

"It's good Renee had you."

"I was glad to help."

I paused. "Can I ask you something?"

"Sure," she replied.

"You said you hadn't had sex in eight years. How is that possible? You're an incredibly attractive woman."

"When you get out of treatment, they strongly encourage you not to date for at least a year so you can focus on yourself and your sobriety. Since then, I've dated a few times, but no one really interested me enough to take the next step."

"It sounds lonely."

"Maybe it was my penance," she whispered.

Her eyes widened, like she hadn't meant to say that out loud.

"Penance for what?" I asked curiously.

"I was a terrible wife, a terrible mother who abandoned her daughter even before Jack kicked me out. By the time I finally admitted I needed help, I was homeless and stealing to support my drug habit. I have a lot to make amends for."

"You've done that now, right? You don't need to keep punishing yourself for the sins of your past."

She shrugged and I took that as a sign she didn't want to answer.

"May I ask what happened? How you started taking drugs? Only if you're comfortable talking about it."

"I was in a car accident, and the doctor prescribed oxycontin. I loved it. It took away the pain and made me feel kind of euphoric. Whenever I stopped taking it, the pain would come back, and I would get really depressed. The doctor kept prescribing them, but after a while even that wasn't enough. I needed more and more to get the same results."

"That sounds hard."

"Eventually I started using alcohol to supplement the drugs. Soon nothing was more important than the drugs, not my daughter, not my husband, not my job. Jack begged me to go to treatment several times, but I blew him off. Eventually he divorced me and got full custody of April. I took off and lived on the streets for a while, never calling April or showing up for my visitation days. I lived that way for a long time until things finally got bad enough for me to realize I needed help. I did six months of in-patient and have been clean ever since. It's been eight years."

I gave her a squeeze. "That's pretty freaking amazing."

She shrugged. "It was the hardest thing I've ever done, but I'm finally in a good place now."

"I'm glad."

We lapsed into silence for a while and eventually Erika's breathing evened out, letting me know that she'd fallen asleep. As I snuggled her into my side, I resolved to do whatever I could to keep her with me forever.

Erika

"Mom, you look beautiful."

I looked up from where the team was finishing my hair and make-up.

Suzanne, April's stepmother, added, "You really do."

I sent her a grateful smile. Suzanne had taken care of my family after I left, and she'd done an excellent job raising my daughter. She was a good match for my ex-husband, and I liked her a lot. She was a kind-hearted soul who'd welcomed me back into the family when I first reached out to Jack and April. I owed her a debt of gratitude.

"Thank you both. But you're the star here, April. It's your special day."

My daughter looked luminous in an off-white mermaid dress that hugged her long, lean figure. It was an off-the-shoulder design with a belted waist and was paired with a ruby necklace her father had given her. Her long brown hair, the same shade as mine, was pulled up in an elegant twist, and the make-up artist had given her a smoky eye and red lips that matched her necklace. It wasn't the lipstick that she'd sent me and Reed out to get, I noted with a shake of my head. Reed had been right about her making up that errand to push us together. Regardless of her lip color, my little girl looked amazing.

I walked towards my daughter and handed her a small box that I'd tucked into my clutch.

"This is for you." I suddenly felt self-conscious. "It's a wedding present. I mean, if you want it."

"Oh Mom, thank you! That's so sweet."

"You don't even know what it is yet," I teased.

April opened the box, revealing an ankle bracelet with little blue stones.

"It's an ankle bracelet," I explained. "I thought it could be your something new and something blue," I told her, referring to the old bride's saying. I'd seen it in the window of a jewelry store a few months ago and had immediately fallen in love with it.

She threw her arms around me and gave me a big hug.

"Mom! I love it! Thank you so much!"

The wedding planner bustled over. "Let me put that on you so you don't crease your dress."

I held April's skirt out of the way while she fastened the jewelry on my daughter's ankle. It fit perfectly.

"Perfect!" the wedding planner decreed. "It's a beautiful piece."

April held her ankle out, showing the bracelet to the other bridesmaids and Suzanne. They oohed and ahhed over it and I felt a rush of relief that it was something she liked. It meant a lot to me to be included in April's wedding, and I'd wanted to give her the perfect gift.

"Okay Moms, it's time to get seated," the wedding planner announced. Suzanne and I each gave April a hug, then headed out towards the wedding chapel area.

Reed was waiting for me just outside. He looked completely dashing in an expensive dark black suit with a thin blue tie. The suit fit him perfectly, as if it had been made just for him. Maybe it had been. His hair was slicked back neatly, and his beard was freshly trimmed. He gave me a smile that damn near melted my panties off.

"You look incredible," he told me sincerely.

I'd gone with a jewel toned blue dress that coincidentally was almost the same shade as his tie. It was an A-line design with a sweetheart neckline, cap sleeves, and a fitted waist. The skirt puffed out a bit before hitting me just below the knee. I'd paired the dress with black shoes with a chunky heel. Like April, the hairstylist had pulled my hair up into a sophisticated twist, with tendrils of hair framing my face.

"Thanks, I haven't looked this good since my own wedding." I smiled and smoothed down his tie. "You're looking pretty handsome yourself."

He gave me a quick hug, and I inhaled the spicy scent of his cologne.

We sat together in the second row, right behind Renee, Jack, and Suzanne. Jonathon's siblings sat next to us.

The minute the ceremony started the tears came. Reed silently handed me tissue after tissue that he'd stuffed in his pocket. For someone who'd never had a serious relationship, he was particularly thoughtful.

The wedding went off without a hitch, and afterwards the family and wedding party went outside to take photos. The sky was darkening with twilight by the time we came back into the ballroom for the reception.

I picked at my dinner, not really feeling hungry. My mind was swirling with emotions between the wedding and what was happening with Reed. We were all going home tomorrow, and I couldn't help but wonder if I'd see Reed again. If I wanted to see him again.

In retrospect, it was foolhardy of me to start something with him knowing that we'd likely run into each other at family events. And yet, everything felt so natural with him, and that freaked me out even more. I'd been in love once before, and I'd ruined it. Even though Jack and April had emerged largely unscathed, I couldn't help but wonder if I really had it in me to have a successful relationship. Maybe I was too damaged. Maybe I had too much baggage.

And maybe he doesn't want more than a fling anyway, the voice in my head suggested. Yet my mind kept going back to when he'd said he was "all in", and when he'd asked me about dating once we were back in the city.

"Penny for your thoughts?"

I looked over at Reed, who was watching me intently. We'd been seated next to each other for the wedding dinner, April's doing I was sure. Not that I minded. Reed was a charming and witty conversationalist, and I could talk to him all night.

I shook my head at his question.

"Just being sentimental." It was partly true.

We were interrupted by the announcement of the newlywed dance. Reed took my hand and pulled me towards the dance floor to watch April and Jonathon have their first dance as a married couple. My daughter looked radiant as she moved around the floor with her new husband. For his part, Jonathon looked like he'd just won the lottery jackpot.

As we watched them dance, Reed moved behind me, wrapping his arms around my waist and pulling me into his chest, the way he'd done on the dock last night. I leaned into his warmth, my head against his shoulder, enjoying the feeling of being protected. It had been a long time.

The music changed, and other people moved to join the newlyweds on the dance floor.

"Do you want to dance?" Reed whispered in my ear.

"Okay."

Normally I wasn't one for dancing, but with Reed it felt natural to turn into his arms and start swaying to the music.

After dancing two slow songs, faster music came on and we returned to our table. The noise level increased, the guests losing their inhibitions with the help of the open bar.

"Does it bother you when people drink around you?" Reed asked curiously.

I shook my head.

"Not at all."

It was true. It felt a little weird to be around people drinking, only because I wasn't one to go to a bar. Most of my friends were in recovery like me, and we found other ways to have fun that didn't involve drinking. But I knew we were not typical by any means.

The reception was crowded and noisy, and the up-tempo music they'd switched to was giving me a headache.

"I'm going to say goodbye to April and go back to my cabin."

Reed looked at me curiously.

"Are you okay?"

I nodded.

"Yeah, but it's been a big day and it's super loud in here. I'm starting to get a headache."

"Would you like some company?" he asked hopefully. "I've been told I give a great scalp massage."

I told myself I should refuse his offer, but I was selfish. I wanted one last night with him. One more time to remember him by. I decided to go for it. But first, I needed to settle myself. My emotions were all over the place between the wedding and how I felt about Reed.

"I need a little time to myself so I can meditate. But can we hook up in about an hour?"

"Sure. Your cabin or mine?"

"I'll come to you."

He pressed a quick kiss against my lips. "See you soon, love."

Reed

I paced back and forth in my cabin, hoping Erika was still planning to come over. Things seemed fine with her while we were dancing, but afterwards it felt like she was pulling away from me. Hopefully, it was just her headache. I still didn't have her phone number so I couldn't call her.

I breathed a sigh of relief when I heard a soft knock on the door. I'd never been so torn up about a woman before, but then again, no woman had ever felt so important to me before.

I opened the door to find Erika standing there, looking like a vision. She'd washed off her make-up and changed into yoga pants and an oversized tee shirt, but her hair was still up in the fancy updo she'd gotten for the wedding.

"Sorry I'm late, I got caught up in my meditation."

"No problem." I walked into the cabin and called over my shoulder, "Do you want something to drink?"

When she didn't answer, I turned around and caught my breath. Erika had pulled off her pants and shirt and was standing there totally nude. I loved how confident she was in her body. She was all soft curves and lean muscle.

I ripped off my shirt and stalked towards her, backing her up against the wall. As soon as I was close enough, she unbuckled my belt and unzipped my pants, letting them fall towards my ankles.

Licking her lips, she slid her little hands into the waistband of my boxers and started stroking my dick. I yanked my underwear down, kicking my clothing behind me, and grabbed her thighs, lifting her up and pressing her against the wall with my body.

She wrapped her legs around my waist. Our mouths met and I kissed her deeply, rolling my rock hard cock against her core.

When we broke for breath Erika gave me a look that was pure need.

"I need you Reed. Now."

I lined myself up with her channel and pushed in slowly, staring into her eyes the entire time. When I bottomed out inside her, I slid back slowly, almost all the way out, then pushed back in with a hard punch of my hips. I repeated the motion several times, until we were both panting with need.

Erika's fingernails dug into my shoulders, holding on as I sped up, feeling almost crazy with the need to stake my claim on her. I lowered my head and sucked on the skin of her shoulder.

One of her hands slid between us, plucking her clit, and then I felt Erika's body tighten around me as her orgasm rolled through her body.

"Reed!"

Her eyes screwed up tight as she shook against the wall. I pumped into her a few more times until I felt the tingling at the base of my spine.

"I'm coming," I grunted just as I released my seed inside her.

I dropped my head to the crook of her neck, breathing heavily as my body recovered. When I finally stepped back, Erika lowered her feet to the floor and gave me a quick peck on the lips.

"Two points for not injuring either of us there," she said.

"I noticed that you haven't gotten hurt since we started sleeping together," I pointed out. "I think my cock is magic."

She rolled her eyes and headed towards the bathroom to clean up. When she returned I was sitting on the bed, leaning against the headboard. I patted the space next to me and she settled in next to me. I wrapped my arm around her and kissed the top of her head.

"It was a good day."

"Yes, the wedding was beautiful," she said. "I'm so glad I was invited."

It wasn't the first time she'd expressed this sense that her relationship with her daughter was tenuous, or that she was surprised to be included in the festivities.

"Of course you got invited," I told her. "April loves you. And you're the one she went to when she was having doubts this morning, right?

Not her father, not her stepmother, not Renee, but you. That means something, doesn't it?"

Erika nodded, her expression contemplative.

"You don't have to do penance forever," I told her, referencing our conversation earlier. "Your family has forgiven you. The question is, when are you going to forgive yourself?"

"Hmm, maybe you're right."

"I'm pretty much always right," I teased. "You'll have to get used to that if we're going to be together."

"Huh?"

We were leaving tomorrow and even though we both lived in the same city, it suddenly felt very important that I settle things between us.

"Erika, I really like you. I've never felt such an intense connection to someone before. I'm hoping we can keep seeing each other once we're back in New York."

She stiffened. "I'm not sure that's a good idea. We come from vastly different worlds, Reed."

"So?"

I turned my head to meet her eyes. They were wary as she suggested, "Why don't we just take it day by day and see how it goes?"

I debated arguing with her, then realized that we had time. She was clearly pushing me off, but we didn't need to settle everything tonight. If I pushed her too far before she was ready, I knew instinctively she would retreat. She didn't think she deserved love, that much was clear, but I was determined to show her that she was wrong. I was already head over heels in love with her, but given that we lived in the same city, we had time to work it out. I could give her a little space to come to terms with what was happening between us.

"You got it, angel. Are you ready for round two?"

Erika

"Well, how was the wedding?"

I smiled as my friend Marjorie stuck her head into my office.

"It was beautiful. A perfect day."

Marjorie came in and dropped into one of the chairs that were set up for my sessions with clients. I moved from behind my desk to join her.

"Lemme see the pictures," she said, making grabby hands at my phone.

I smiled and opened my Facebook app where wedding guests had posted candid pictures on April's profile. She scrolled through with a smile.

"April looked beautiful. And that Jonathon is a handsome kid."

"Totally."

"Wow. Erika. I've never seen you look so fancy."

I looked down at a photo someone had taken of me with April. I had to admit that I did look good. In my job I usually dressed casually because many of our clients were put off by counselors who dressed up. It was easier to connect with people when you were wearing jeans and a shirt instead of something more corporate looking.

Marjorie scrolled again, then her head snapped up.

"And who is this handsome man, young lady? He looks familiar."

Someone had captured a picture of me and Reed dancing. We were dancing close, our faces mere inches away as we stared into each other's eyes. In the next shot, we were sitting at a table, talking and laughing. I had to admit, we looked good together.

"That's Reed. He's Jonathon's uncle."

"Reed Nelson? The CEO of Nelson Financial?"

"I guess?"

We hadn't really talked about Reed's work that much. He'd mentioned that he worked in finance, managing people's money, and April had told me that he was wealthy, but that's really all I knew. I didn't realize he was a CEO or that he owned his own company.

"You hooked up with a billionaire at the wedding?"

"What?" I stared at my friend in confusion.

"Reed Nelson is one of Manhattan's elite. Here...."

She tapped a few times, opening a browser and clicking. She handed me the phone and I scrolled through articles about Reed's net worth, pictures of him with socialites, and attending charity dinners with actors and famous sports figures.

"This says he's only a millionaire," I pointed out, as if that made a difference. I'd already thought that Reed was out of my league, but I hadn't realized just how far out of my league he actually was. I'd had reservations about being with him before I knew that he was the kind of person that reporters took pictures of.

As if he'd somehow knew we were talking about him, my phone dinged with a text.

Reed: *Hey there, angel. Did you get home okay?*

I felt a stab of guilt. Reed had texted me last night and I'd never responded. My mind had been swirling about him the entire ride home from Mountain Ridge Resort. When I got home I'd gone for a run and deep cleaned my apartment trying to work through my nervous energy. Usually, I tried really hard not to avoid my problems, but yesterday was an exception. After I'd woken up in Reed's arms, I'd packed my stuff and hightailed it out of Virginia like I was running from the cops.

Erika: *Yes, thanks. Sorry, I meant to text you back and lost track of time.*

Reed: *How about dinner tonight?*

Erika: *I don't think that's a good idea.*

Reed: *Is everything ok?*

Erika: *Sorry, I've got to go, I'm working now.*

I looked up to see Marjorie watching me. Her gaze was sharp. She was my best friend, and she knew me better than anyone. It was hard to hide things from her when she set her mind to something.

"Is that him texting you?" she asked with a teasing smile.

"Yeah."

"Are you going to see him again?" she asked curiously.

"I haven't decided."

"Girl, if I got myself a good-looking millionaire who looked at me the way he's looking at you in those pictures...well, I would grab onto him for sure. Love doesn't come around every day, especially at our age."

Marjorie left and I spent longer than I would admit staring blankly at my computer and thinking about Reed instead of tackling the mound of paperwork I needed to get through.

I'd had a terrible time sleeping last night, and around two in the morning I realized it was because I missed Reed. I couldn't believe it. We'd only slept together for two nights, but somehow I missed having his big body curled around mine. Needless to say, that had freaked me out. I'd gotten up and done some meditation, which relaxed me enough to finally fall into a fitful sleep.

I got through the rest of my workday on autopilot and headed home to the comfort of my little apartment. It was a tiny one-bedroom, but it was rent controlled, and I'd lived there for about five years. One of the things I liked best was having a doorman. It provided a level of security that I appreciated as a woman living alone in the city.

A familiar figure was leaning against the desk when I entered the lobby of my building.

"Reed."

The man who'd dominated my thoughts since I left Mountain Ridge stood there looking every inch the successful businessman in a navy pinstriped suit, red tie, and God help me, a vest. I was a sucker for a guy in a vest.

"Hey."

His voice was soft, his eyes searching mine with a look of uncertainty that I'd never seen from him. He lifted up an arm to show me a paper bag.

"I brought Chinese. I was hoping we could talk."

I wasn't surprised he was here. I knew my response to his dinner invitation was a bit curt. Rude even. Even via text he was astute enough to know that I was giving him the brush-off. Looking at him, standing in my lobby looking so tall and handsome, I had a hard time remembering why I thought that was a good idea to avoid him.

"How did you get my address?" I asked.

"April."

I really needed to talk to my daughter about respecting people's privacy.

"Is this guy bothering you, Miss Stone?" the doorman asked. It broke me out of my stupor.

"No, it's fine Jimmy. Thank you for checking."

"Come on up," I told Reed, my tone weary.

He followed me to the elevator. We stood side by side in the little box as it carried us up to my floor. Neither of us spoke, but I could feel the tension between us. My mind was churning. Things had felt so good between us at Mountain Ridge, but now we were back in the real world. The world where Reed was a wealthy businessman, and I was a lowly alcohol and drug counselor with a minor criminal record and a sketchy past.

I let Reed into my apartment, and he looked around curiously. I tried to see my apartment through his eyes. It was small, neat as a pin, with a plain beige couch I'd picked up at a thrift store. The walls were the boring off white that they'd been when I'd moved in and somehow I'd never gotten around to putting up any pictures on the walls.

Seeing it through fresh eyes, I could see that it was kind of austere. Other than the framed picture on the side table of me and April that she'd given me for Christmas last year, there was no hint of who lived here. I wondered why I'd never noticed how bland and boring my apartment was. When I'd slipped and told Reed I was doing penance for the people I'd hurt, I hadn't realized how much it was true everywhere in my life.

"Are you hungry?" he asked, his voice cautious.

"Sure."

I wasn't really hungry, but it seemed polite since he'd brought food. He followed me into the kitchen.

"What do you want to drink?" I asked. "I have water, diet coke, or orange juice."

"Water is fine."

I turned and started walking just as Reed opened a cabinet to look for plates. The cabinet door opened too quickly, and it hit me square in the face. I jumped back with a squeak, gripping my cheek.

"Oh crap! I'm so sorry, I didn't know that would happen." Reed looked appalled. "Are you okay?"

I shot him a wry look. "I see you're back to trying to kill me."

Reed

I wondered what it meant that whenever we were fighting this pull between us, we were accident prone? The universe was clearly telling us to be together. I reached out and stroked Erika's cheek with my fingers. It was a little red from where the corner of the door had caught her, but nothing serious.

She leaned into my hand and our eyes met.

"I've missed you," I whispered.

"We saw each other yesterday morning," she reminded me softly. Her eyes looked huge in her pale face, a little shadowed underneath, as if she hadn't slept. I could see the emotion swirling in the brown depths.

"Let's talk and eat," I suggested, wanting to lighten the mood a bit.

We ate in silence for a few minutes, Erika picking at her food. I was coming to realize that was something she did when she was uncomfortable.

"It feels like you're avoiding me. Is something wrong?" I asked. "Did I do something to upset you?"

Her gaze shot up to mine.

"No, not at all."

"I like you Erika, I really like you, and I think we could have something great here. But I feel like you're pulling away," I said.

We'd spent a fabulous night together after the wedding but when we'd gotten up yesterday morning, Erika had seemed distant. She'd rushed around to leave my cabin, refusing my offer for breakfast, saying she needed to get back to the city.

I'd run into April and Jonathon having breakfast in the main restaurant. They shared that April had popped over to say goodbye to them and then headed out.

"What's going on with you two?" April had asked. *"I thought things were going well but she seemed really rushed to leave this morning."*

"I think she's freaking out," I'd told April. "I love her. I know it sounds ridiculous when we've only known each other a few days, but I've had enough experience with the wrong women to know when I've found the right one."

"Aww, that's so great," April gushed. "But the thing about my mom is, she's kept herself distant from everyone since we reconnected. It's like she's afraid to get too close. She acted shocked that I invited her to the wedding, as if I wouldn't invite my own mother. She needs to...I guess she just needs to know that it's okay to receive love again, you know? I'm not sure if she's afraid to hurt us, or afraid of getting hurt herself."

"Yeah, I get that."

"If you really love her, you're going to need to fight for her. Convince her to take a chance."

"I'm not pulling away," Erika denied, pulling my attention back to the present. "We're back to real life now. I have a job and responsibilities and you have your company to run and your galas to attend."

My eyes narrowed. That was a weird thing to say. I wondered if she'd googled me. I'd been at an event at the Met last month, and I knew there were pictures of that on the internet.

"What are you talking about?"

She sighed and set her chopsticks down on her plate.

"Look Reed, I had a great time with you at Mountain Ridge, injuries aside, and I like you too. Too much, maybe. But that was all a vacation bubble. In the real world, we don't fit. You're a wealthy CEO and me, well, I'm just a counselor who lives in a one-bedroom apartment and buys most of her clothes at Target. I'm not the woman you take to some fancy event at the Met."

Yep, she'd definitely googled me.

"I don't think this is about our careers or going to the Met, I think this is about you being afraid."

"I'm not afraid!" she protested.

"I don't pretend to understand everything you've gone through, Erika, but here's what I see. You've been successful in your recovery for many years, you've been back in a relationship with your family, you have a good job, you have people who love you, but it's like you're still punishing yourself for everything that happened in the past. If April and Jack can forgive you, why can't you forgive yourself?"

"I have."

"Are you sure? Because the thing is, it doesn't seem that way."

I paused, then looked her straight in the eye so she could see my sincerity. "I love you Erika."

She gasped.

"You can't love me."

"Sure I can. You're very lovable. You're the only one who doesn't see that."

Erika pushed up from the table and began pacing. I already knew her well enough to know that she used physical activity to help her work things through, so I continued to eat my lemon chicken while she paced. Her lips were moving, as if she was talking to herself. She returned to the table a full three minutes later, looking a little bit calmer. It was fascinating to watch.

"Are you saying you want us to date?" she asked.

"I'm saying I want forever with you Erika, but yes, that would start with dating. Unless you want to move in with me right now?"

Her head snapped up, her face so appalled that I burst out laughing.

"Relax. I was kidding. All I'm asking is that you don't shut me out, that you don't let external bullshit get in the way of what we both want. Let's spend some time getting to know each other better and when the time is right, when we both feel ready, we can take the next step."

Of course I was ready right now, but I kept that to myself. Instead, I reached across the table and wrapped her small hand in mine.

"I've waited my whole life to meet someone like you. I've never been in love before. It scares the hell out of me, but it also feels right. I get it if you're not there yet, but if you also see a future with us, we owe it to ourselves to explore what looks like."

When she didn't answer I added, "Take a chance Erika. Take a chance on me, take a chance on a relationship, and most importantly, take a chance on yourself."

She stared at me for a long moment before she finally nodded. "Okay."

"Really?" My heart lifted in my chest.

She gave me a smile that loosened up the tightness I'd felt in my chest ever since she'd run off yesterday morning.

"But I think I'd better increase my health insurance coverage if I'm going to spend more time with you."

"I think you'll be fine now. We'll both be fine. You only get injured when you're trying to avoid me."

"That's not technically true. I didn't even know you when you hit me with your car."

"I didn't hit you," I reminded her. "You hit my car with your body, remember?"

She rolled her eyes. I strode around the table and pulled her up to standing.

"How about you show me your bedroom?"

Her smile turned coy.

"You bring me Chinese takeout and you think that means you're going to get lucky?" she asked.

"I already am lucky, angel. I've got you."

Epilogue – Erika

"Welcome to Mountain Ridge Resort."

I smiled at the clerk as Reed gave his name.

"I see you're here for one of our wedding packages. Congratulations."

"Thanks," I said. "We met here last year, so it seemed fitting to come back for our wedding."

"Mom! Reed!"

We turned to see April and Jonathon heading towards us. My daughter looked radiant, with no indication of the fact that she was pregnant. She'd told me the big news two days ago, swearing me to secrecy. She planned to tell Jonathon tonight, thinking it would be special to tell him at the same place they'd gotten married.

I couldn't believe how much had changed in the last year. I'd gone back into therapy, and that had helped me navigate the changes in my life, including entering into my first serious relationship since my divorce. Reed had been right about one thing: while my family had forgiven me, I still needed to forgive myself

My daughter and I had grown closer as I started to trust our relationship more. I'd felt better about letting April in, and we were spending more time together. I was grateful every day for the gift of her forgiveness, but I no longer feared that she'd take it back if she got angry with me. Her love for me wasn't any more conditional than mine was for her.

And then there was Reed. We'd dated for three months before he convinced me to move in with him. After so many years living alone, it had been a big adjustment for both of us, but we'd weathered the transition like we did everything: with open communication and a sense of humor.

We had dinner together every night and had spent a lot of time exploring our common interests. We'd even started running together every morning.

Six months ago, he'd proposed to me. I'd never in a million years thought I'd get married again, but with Reed it all felt like it was meant to be. We were having a very small wedding. April and Jonathon were standing up for us, and we'd also invited Renee and her new man, Renee's kids, my two best friends Marjorie and Sue, and oddly enough, Jack and Suzanne.

Somehow my ex-husband and I had become good friends again, and Reed and I sometimes joined him and his wife for game nights or a dinner out. It was probably weird to other people that I hung out with my ex-husband and his wife, but the four of us really got along great.

We got the keys from the girl at the desk and walked to our cabin. As we headed down the shaded path, I breathed in the fresh air and the smell of the trees, such a big change from the city. We got to the Forestview cabin, the same one Reed had stayed in last time, and he scanned the key card.

"Should I carry you over the threshold?"

I laughed. "I think you're supposed to do that after the wedding."

He dropped his bag and picked me up. "Let's practice."

He turned, narrowly missing knocking my head into the doorframe.

"I swear to God, if you give me a bruise for my wedding pictures, I will kill you."

He tossed me on the bed then stalked back to the entryway to pull in the bags and close the door. Then he rushed back to me, pulling off his shirt.

"What are you doing?" I laughed.

"More practice."

He dropped his pants and slid his boxers down his legs.

"I think this is one thing we don't need to practice," I told him. Our sex life was healthy and had shown no signs of slowing down, despite being together for a year now.

He leapt on the bed, making me bounce, and I laughed again. That was one thing about Reed: I had laughed more with him in the last year than I had the entire previous ten years combined. He was funny and charming, but also thoughtful and attentive. I really was a lucky woman.

I pushed him to his back and laid on top of him, bracing myself on my elbows to look down at him. I could feel his cock growing beneath me.

"Have I told you lately that I love you?"

His eyes darkened. He was definitely the more demonstrative of the two of us, but I'd been getting better at the lovey dovey stuff. I knew it was important to him.

"I can never hear that enough, angel."

"I love you, Reed Nelson, now let's practice for the honeymoon."

***

Did you like this book? Show the love and leave me a review. Reviews are like puppies, they make you feel happy.

Keep reading for a special excerpt from "Until You Came Along", available everywhere now.

About the Mountain Ridge Resort Series

Summer is the season for love at Mountain Ridge Resort! Pack your bags and get ready to have the time of your life at this charming, lakeside resort nestled in the Virginia mountains. This summer, our guests are getting much more than they expect, when what starts as a summer getaway ends in love and happily-ever-after! Your reservation is confirmed. Check in today, and join some of your favorite romance authors for twenty-five unforgettable, steamy, summer love stories.

RESORTING TO LOVE by Karla Doyle
mybook.to/ResortingKD [1]
SUMMER SAVORY by Bree Weeks
mybook.to/SavoryBW [2]
THE RELUCTANT HOLIDAY by Katharine O'Neill
mybook.to/ReluctantKO [3]
HOLIDAY RIDE by Emma Bray
mybook.to/RideEB [4]
SUMMER LANE by Andie Fenichel
mybook.to/SummerLaneAF [5]
HOLIDAY HEAT by Tamrin Banks
mybook.to/HolidayHeatTB [6]
ONE HOT SUMMER by Mae Harden
mybook.to/HotSummerMH [7]
SUMMER MUSE by Ember Davis
mybook.to/MuseED [8]

---

1. http://mybook.to/ResortingKD

2. http://mybook.to/SavoryBW

3. http://mybook.to/ReluctantKO

4. http://mybook.to/RideEB

5. http://mybook.to/SummerLaneAF

6. http://mybook.to/HolidayHeatTB

7. http://mybook.to/HotSummerMH

HIS FOR THE SUMMER by Sammi Starlight
mybook.to/HisSummerSS [9]
SUMMER STORM by Matilda Martel
mybook.to/SummerStormMM [10]
MOUNTAIN MAID by Violet Rae
mybook.to/MaidVR [11]
SUMMER HATE by Melissa Ivers
mybook.to/HateMI [12]
RESORT HEAT by MK Moore
mybook.to/HeatMKM [13]
THE LAST SUMMER by Ava Pearl
mybook.to/LastSummerAP [14]
HOLIDAY PROPOSAL by Lana Love
mybook.to/ProposalLL [15]
FAUX HOLIDAY by Kylie Marcus
mybook.to/FauxKM [16]
RESORTING TO A ROCKSTAR by Stormi Wilde
mybook.to/RockstarSW [17]
HOLIDAY WITH HER BILLIONAIRE BOSS by Imani Jay
mybook.to/HolidayBossIJ [18]
HIGH STAKES HOLIDAY by Jailaa West

---

8.   http://mybook.to/MuseED

9.   http://mybook.to/HisSummerSS

10.   http://mybook.to/SummerStormMM

11.   http://mybook.to/MaidVR

12.   http://mybook.to/HateMI

13.   http://mybook.to/HeatMKM

14.   http://mybook.to/LastSummerAP

15.   http://mybook.to/ProposalLL

16.   http://mybook.to/FauxKM

17.   http://mybook.to/RockstarSW

18.   http://mybook.to/HolidayBossIJ

mybook.to/StakesJW [19]
HOLIDAY HEARTS by Carly Keene
mybook.to/HeartsCK [20]
SUMMER WEDDING by Rose Bak
mybook.to/WeddingRB [21]
HOT AUGUST NIGHTS by Khloe Summers
mybook.to/NightsKS [22]
SUMMER CHANCES by Lisa Freed
mybook.to/ChancesLF [23]
SUMMER LOVIN' by Kameron Claire
mybook.to/LovinKC [24]
ONE NIGHT WITH A MOUNTAIN MAN by Eve London
mybook.to/MountainEL [25]

---

19.   http://mybook.to/StakesJW

20.   http://mybook.to/HeartsCK

21.   http://mybook.to/WeddingRB

22.   http://mybook.to/NightsKS

23.   http://mybook.to/ChancesLF

24.   http://mybook.to/LovinKC

25.   http://mybook.to/MountainEL

Special Preview

Until You Came Along by Rose Bak

Jen heard the rumbling from all the way in the kitchen. Wiping her hands on a towel, she walked to the front porch to watch the two large buses drive up the long driveway to the farmhouse. Belching smoke, they idled and came to a stop, one behind the other.

Although it wasn't even 10 a.m. yet, the sun shone brightly in the summer sky, showcasing the dust left in the wake of the parked buses. A bird squawked loudly in the sudden silence as a serious looking young woman scurried out of the first bus, glasses askew, a clipboard gripped in one hand, cellphone in another. Two large mountains of men followed her, hulking shadows.

"Jen Oliver? The band is here. We'll just come in and...." she moved to enter the house, but Jen stood her ground, blocking the door.

"Where are they?" she asked the woman, her tone icy. "And who are you exactly?"

The woman looked flustered for a brief moment before her stern mask fell back down again. She shuffled her cell phone into the hand with the clipboard and stuck out her now-free hand to shake. "I'm Simone. I manage the band."

Jen ignored her hand. "Well, manage them out of those buses. They don't get to send the help out to greet their sister."

Simone looked confused as she dropped her hand back to her side. "They're all sleeping. They had a late night. We'll just come in and check...."

"Still up all night and sleeping all day, huh? That's been the same since they were teenagers." Jen shook her head. On the farm they had all been taught the value of hard work – up before dawn, work all day, and early to bed. Somehow those lessons hadn't really stuck with her brothers despite her grandparents' best efforts over the years.

79

Of course, the boys, as she still thought of them, had been away from the farm for ten years now, chasing fame and fortune as the biggest boy band to hit the charts since N Sync. Like the band that came before them, the Oliver Boys had grown up but continued to en-chant teenage girls across the world with their pop tunes.

Simone clearly felt protective of the boys. "They played last night in Wichita you know," she said sternly. "The show went until almost mid-night, then they met the fans and press for hours after."

"By meet the fans and press do you mean got drunk and partied?" Jen's tone did little to hide her opinion of the boys and their reputation for debauched partying.

Simone shook her head. "They've mostly settled down now. There's not as much partying as there used to be when they were younger. But they still need to make an effort to meet people, it's part of the job. Now we'll just come in and...."

Jen shook her head. "Well," she drawled. "When they wake up from their so-called job, you send them on in. The rest of you need to find some other place to bunk. I'm not running a hotel for drunken roadies here."

A slight movement behind Simone caught Jen's eyes. One of the giant men flanking Simone shook with repressed laughter, his mouth twisted in a smirk but his face otherwise impassive. Jen looked at him for the first time. He was the size of a small tank, several inches over six feet tall, with impossibly wide shoulders and large biceps. His hair was a dark blond, "dishwater blonde" her grandma would call it, worn mil-itary short. He was dressed all in black, and she noticed a gun on the shoulder holster. Jen wondered why he felt he needed a gun out here in the middle of nowhere. She felt him watching her and she raised her eyes to his, a shiver of awareness coursing through her, although she couldn't make out his eyes behind the dark sunglasses.

"Miss Oliver..." Simone started again.

"Jen"

"OK, then, Jen, we need to do a security sweep before the boys come in. If you could just move aside, we'll get started." Simone nodded decisively.

"A security—-what the hell are you talking about?"

Simone turned to the man who'd been staring at Jen earlier. "This is Nick, he's head of security for the band. He'll be doing a security sweep and assessment with Brian here," she pointed at the second silent man.

"We don't need a security sweep. This place is as safe as it comes. We don't even lock the doors in these parts."

Simone shook her head again, vibrating with irritation and clearly not used to people disobeying her orders. "No way. The boys don't go anywhere without a security check ahead of time. I'm afraid I have to insist."

Jen shot her a look filled with venom, her tone as cold as ice. "You can insist all you like but this is my property. You have no right to it, and neither do the boys. Y'all can just run along now, I'm not having some ginormous strangers poking around my property. Don't make me sic the dogs on you." Simone's mouth dropped open.

This was an empty threat. Jen's three dogs looked mean, but they were incurably friendly. They were just as likely to lick a person to death as bite them. Jen had a sneaking suspicion that if someone tried to kill her the dogs would jump over her body and leave with the killer. But these music people didn't need to know that. If there was one thing Jen hated, it was music people. They were way too self-important and proud.

"Excuse me ma'am," the guy called Nick interrupted.

"Jen," she repeated, a trace of irritation in her tone.

He inclined his head. "Sorry. Jen. As Simone mentioned, I'm head of security for the band. We've had some issues and I would be very appreciative if my team could just poke around for a bit and make sure there's nothing amiss." His tone was deferential and charming, which only heightened Jen's suspicions.

"What kind of issues?"

"I'm afraid I'm not at liberty to discuss that ma—I mean Jen."

"Then I'm afraid I'm not at liberty to grant you access to my property. You step foot off that driveway, and I'll shoot you myself, right after I set the dogs on you. And you," she pointed at Simone, "better make sure no one bothers me again until I see those boys on my porch." She spun on her heel and slammed the door. It was going to be a long day.

***

For more of Jen's story, check out Until You Came Along by Rose Bak. Available at select online retailers.

Other Books by Rose Bak

Boozy Book Club Series
Beach Reads
Bubbly & Billionaires
Martinis & Mysteries
Bourbon & Bikers
The Good with Numbers Holiday Romance Series
Love Unmasked
The Thanksgiving Scrooge
Maid for Christmas
Countdown to Love
Valentine's Lottery
Bite-Sized Shifters Paranormal Romance Series
Long Distance Wolf
Wolf Doctor
Kat's Dog
Designer Wolf
Wolf Sheriff
Cocktail Wolf
Second Chance Wolf
The Oliver Boys Band Contemporary Romance Series
Until You Came Along
Rock Star Teacher
Rock Star Writer
Rock Star Neighbor
Rock Star Lawyer
Loving the Holidays Contemporary Romance Series
Dating Santa
New Year's Steve
Independence Dave
Comfort & Joy

Holidays with the Shifters Series
Santa's Claws
Bear Humbug
Jingle Bear
Silver Paws
Joy to the Wolf
Lion's Heart
The Diamond Bay Contemporary Romance Series
Brand New Penny
Fresh as a Daisy
Right as Rain
Reunited Series
Together Again
Finding My Baby
Standalones
Beach Wedding
Jessie's Girl
Summer Wedding
Non-fiction
What to Do If You Find a Cougar in Your Living Room: Self-Care in an Uncaring World

It's All About Relationships: Reflections on Love, Friendship, and Connection

Catch up with these and other stories coming soon. Join my newsletter for more information[1] or follow my author page on your favorite retailer.

---

1. *https://storyoriginapp.com/giveaways/62ee758e-068f-11eb-904e-c373f6014fe1*

About the Author

Rose Bak has been obsessed with books since she got her first library card at age five. She is a passionate reader with an e-reader bursting with thousands of beloved books.

Although Rose enjoys writing both fiction and nonfiction, romance novels have always been her favorite guilty pleasure, both as a reader and an author. Rose's contemporary romance books focus on strong female characters over thirty-five and the alpha males who love them. Expect a lot of steam, a little bit of snark, and a guaranteed happily ever after.

Rose lives in the Pacific Northwest with her family, and special needs dogs. In addition to writing, she also teaches accessible yoga and loves music. Sadly, she has absolutely no musical talent, so she mostly sings in the shower.

Please sign up for the Rose Bak Romance newsletter[1] to get a free book and keep up to date on all the latest news.

You can also follow Rose on Facebook[2], Instagram[3], Twitter[4], Goodreads[5], or Bookbub[6].

---

1. https://storyoriginapp.com/giveaways/62ee758e-068f-11eb-904e-c373f6014fe1

2. https://www.facebook.com/AuthorRoseBak

3. https://www.instagram.com/authorrosebak/

4. https://twitter.com/AuthorRoseBak

5. https://www.goodreads.com/authorrosebak

6. https://www.bookbub.com/authors/rose-bak

Printed in Great Britain
by Amazon

84552947R10051